TAKE US THERE

A Joy Universe Novel

LOUISA MASTERS

Take Us There

Copyright © 2020 by Louisa Masters

Cover Designer: Reese Dante www.reesedante.com

Editor: Hot Tree Editing

All rights reserved.

Paperback ISBN 978-0-6489776-0-5

Take Us There

Dominic Hurst is a man who's always up for a challenge. Step in as director of the world's second-largest theme park complex? No problem. Clean up the mess the previous director left behind? Sure. Have his seventeen-year-old daughter move in with him in a last-minute custody change? Bring it on.

Face off with a town full of matchmakers? Uh... what?

Oliver Jeffries is a man more than comfortable with his life. Teach teenagers to fall in love with literature? Absolutely. Tackle mindboggling tasks as head of the English department? Pass him the whip. Placate parents convinced their perfect children can do no wrong? Pfft. Child's play.

Agree to a friends-with-benefits arrangement with the most talked-about man in Joyville? Uhm... maybe in secret?

When Dom and Oliver meet, there's no question that friendship won't be enough. But the citizens of

Joyville don't know the meaning of "private," and dating the director puts Oliver firmly in the spotlight.

With the whole town watching and laying bets, is their fledgling relationship doomed to fail?

ONE

Dom

I have a strict no-phones policy in meetings. I've had this policy for myself for twenty-five years—and how fucked-up is it that cell phones have been around so long? I guess I need to stop thinking of myself as still being in my early twenties—and from the moment I achieved enough seniority to enforce it for others, I have. It's impossible to run a meeting efficiently if people are answering calls or texts or even playing games and checking social media.

But that's so rude, I hear you say. *Surely nobody would be playing games on their phone during a meeting.*

Oh, my sweet summer child. Of course they would. People are rude. Or more to the point, they don't consider their own actions rude because they come up with some form of justification. *"That part of the agenda wasn't relevant to me."*

"We went over that same information in another meeting I sat in on."

"He was just reading from the notes we all have anyway."

I don't care. I really don't. If you attend a meeting

I'm running—or these days, a meeting I'm *attending*— your phone gets muted or switched off, and it stays in your pocket.

Why do we care right now? Well, it means I can't check my own phone when it starts to vibrate in my pocket an hour and a half into the half-day strategy session the executive team is having. I'm fine with that. It's my policy.

And then two minutes later, it rings again.

Five minutes after that, a third time.

Ten minutes later, again.

Fuck. The exec team is here in the room with me. My assistant knows where I am and would just come find me if she needed something urgent—and anybody else at the company who can't reach me on my cell would try her next. There aren't many other people who have my cell number. This is either a really persistent telemarketer or an emergency.

And when you have a seventeen-year-old daughter who's always in the thick of things, you fear emergencies.

I wait the longest forty-five seconds of my life for Elise from marketing, who I literally can't stand, to wrap up her latest complaint, then say, "That's certainly something for us all to take on board, thanks, Elise. We'll have to keep it in mind as we're working, and maybe we can come up with a permanent solution. In the meantime, we've been at this for a while now, so why don't we take a quick bathroom break? Back here in ten minutes."

Elise looks like she wants to protest and insist I do more, but the others are already getting up and heading for the door or the coffeemaker on the sideboard. And really, what does she expect? She runs the marketing department. I can understand her getting pissed off when people give no guidance as to what they're looking for and then complain about the campaign they get, but she can't expect everyone to bring her a fully developed campaign concept—if they all had the skills and time to do that, the marketing department would be redundant.

I push back from the table and follow the crowd out, pulling my phone from my pocket as I do. Sure enough, all four missed calls are from the same local number. No messages, which means it could still be a telemarketer. But I have sole care of my daughter right now, so is that a chance I can take?

I wave at my assistant, who's on the phone, as I head toward my office. I have to call this number back.

"...hold on one second. Dom!" Layla hisses, and I pause and turn my head toward her. She's a really fantastic assistant, and she doesn't take that tone very often. "It's Cara's school."

Fuck fuck fuck. I don't bother having her transfer the call over, just cross to her desk and reach for the phone.

"Dominic Hurst."

"Mr. Hurst, this is Edith Hamilton from Joyville High School. Your daughter, Cara, is in my English literature class."

"Is Cara okay?" My heart is in my throat, although honestly, the fact that it's a teacher calling and not the front office is a good thing.

"She's a particularly difficult young lady, Mr. Hurst."

I pause, because that's not what I was asking, and also, if this woman called Cara a "young lady" to her face, then this call is probably because Cara is in trouble for telling her teacher where to go.

"Is Cara safe and well?" I ask pointedly. Edith Hamilton stutters, clearly nonplussed by my non-reaction to her statement.

"As far as I am aware. But—"

"Thank you. Has she been suspended or expelled, or otherwise done anything that requires my immediate presence at the school?"

"Not *immediate*, no. I have a class in ten minutes. But I would like a meeting with you at your earliest convenience. Cara's disruptive and disrespectful attitude in class must be dealt with."

I suck in a deep breath through my nose. "Ms. Hamilton—"

"*Mrs.* Hamilton," she corrects.

"Of course. Mrs. Hamilton, were you the person who tried to reach me on my cell phone four times within the last half hour?"

"I was. And I must say, if you were aware of the calls, it was rather rude of you not to answer."

Is she fucking kidding me?

"And just to be clear, you wanted to reach me in order to set up a meeting, not because of an emergency?"

"This is a very important matter, Mr. Hurst."

"I agree that anything related to my daughter is very important, Mrs. Hamilton. However, as this is not an emergency, I'm unsure why you called four times—five if we count this call to my office—in thirty minutes. Nor did you leave a message asking for me to return your call —any of them."

She begins spluttering again, but I keep talking.

"Is tomorrow afternoon at three thirty suitable for that meeting?" It will mean rearranging my schedule, but as the boss, rearranging my schedule is something I'm able to do.

"I would prefer this afternoon," she says stiffly.

"I'm sorry, I can't get away today if it's not an emergency. And I'd also like the opportunity to speak with Cara before we meet."

I'm not quite sure how to describe the sound she makes. Annoyed? Offended? It's definitely not a good sound.

"Mr. Hurst, I do not appreciate being called a liar."

This can't be real. I mean, seriously...

"I didn't call you a liar, ma'am. If I thought you were a liar, I wouldn't be agreeing to this meeting. Now if you'll excuse me, I have a meeting to get back to. Goodbye." I barely wait for her grumbled goodbye before ending the call.

I am pissed. So, so very pissed.

I close my eyes and force myself to take a deep breath and count to ten. When I open my eyes, Layla is watching me sympathetically.

"She's a piece of work, isn't she?" Layla has four kids, two now in college and two still at Joyville High, and she's familiar with most of the teaching staff.

I shake my head. "She probably has a valid reason to be angry with Cara," I admit. As much as I adore my daughter, she hasn't yet learned that sometimes it's worth losing a battle to win the war. She stands up for everything she believes in—*everything*. And while I fully support her going head-to-head with a teacher who's picking on another student, she needs to learn to suck it up if a teacher assigns homework on a long weekend. It often gets to the point that her teachers dislike her even if they recognize her intelligence and kind heart.

"Maybe," Layla counters, "but she definitely didn't need to be calling here like the school was on fire. Did you say she called your cell four times? For a parent-teacher meeting?" She shakes her head, making her killer Afro sway. "They should have made her retire years ago."

I hesitate. I should be getting back to the board-room, but I sense a story here, one I might need to know. "Tell me quick."

Sure enough, Layla leans forward, the light of gossip in her eyes. "She was one of the first teachers at Joyville High, there the day it opened back when Joyville and Joy Universe were built."

I do a quick calculation. "She must be over eighty, then," I exclaim. "Why hasn't she retired? The poor woman must be exhausted trying to run herd on teenagers all day." Hell, that's not something I'd like to do, and I'm more than thirty years younger than her.

"She's eighty-two this year. And don't feel too sorry for her—she's terrorized every student she ever taught, and lately she's gotten worse. She's been refusing to retire, though, and because her husband was on the school board until he died of a heart attack two years ago—during a school board meeting—she's gotten away with it. I heard a rumor that this will be her last year, but I don't know how true it is."

I sigh. This meeting is going to be so much fun. "Thanks for the tip."

She opens the middle drawer of her desk and pulls out a Snickers bar. "Here. Get on back to the strategy session and try not to worry too much. I'll fix your calendar for tomorrow so you can get away early."

"If you weren't happily married, I would totally scoop you up," I joke, and she grins.

"Every time Marcus pisses me off, I tell him I have options and he'd better look out."

I head back to the boardroom feeling just a bit lighter.

———

CARA'S GOT dinner cooking when I get home a little before seven that evening. That doesn't mean she's sucking up—we have a cleaning service that comes in once a week, and the condo doesn't need any yard work, but other than that, we split chores like cooking, shopping for groceries, and doing laundry evenly between us.

I call out a hello and get one back before going to my bedroom to dump my laptop bag and change out of my work clothes. It's only been six weeks or so since Cara came to live with me, and I like it. When my wife and I split up three years ago, we discussed it with Cara and all decided that she'd divide her time between us. My ex and I both had jobs in the same approximate area of Boston, so I let her have the house—she was always the one who loved it anyway—and I found one in a nearby neighborhood that meant Cara could easily get to school and see her friends when she was staying with me. Then, when I got headhunted for the job of director here at Joy Universe—in the middle of nowhere, southern Georgia—we agreed that Cara would stay with her mom during the school year and come to me during vacations. She only had one year of school left, after all, and I would probably be able to arrange some long weekends to visit her in Boston too. Cara was the driving force for me taking this job when I was hesitant about leaving her. She pointed out that it was a great opportunity, one I'd been working toward for decades, and that she'd be leaving for college in a year anyway. Honestly, her maturity during that conversation impressed and surprised me. I was so used to seeing the Cara who jumped in headfirst to every situation that I forgot how intelligent and thoughtful she is.

So I moved to Georgia in August this year—just three months ago. And then in September, my ex called to tell me that she was being seconded to Japan for a year and that Cara wanted to come live with me so she could have her senior year in America.

I agreed, of course, even though I could hear how upset Tia was about leaving Cara for the year. Truthfully, even though Cara would possibly benefit from the cultural experience of living abroad, if Tia had tried to bring her, I would have fought tooth and nail. Getting up to Boston for a weekend every couple of months is eminently doable. Japan, not so much.

And that's the story of how I currently have sole custody of my seventeen-year-old daughter.

Who I now need to interrogate about the trouble she's allegedly causing in her English lit class.

I go to the kitchen, where Cara has half the table set for dinner and the other half covered with her homework, which she's bent over. The oven is on, and I can smell melting cheese. "Lasagna?" I ask, going to drop a kiss on the top of her head. For a while last year she had her hair super short, basically just a few millimeters of fuzz all over her scalp. I know she loved the convenience of having it that short, and it really brought out the striking bone structure she got from her mother, but the chin length she has it now reminds me of how it was when she was a little girl. Although it wasn't sapphire then.

"Eggplant parma," she replies absently while she finishes writing a sentence, then she looks up and smiles at me. "How was work?"

I shrug as I take the seat next to her. "Productive. We're making a lot of headway into plans for the future, and things are picking up across the company. This was the right move for me."

"You're welcome," she teases, but when I don't laugh, she winces. "Mrs. Hamilton called you, didn't she?"

"Five times," I confirm. "I thought you were in an accident or something."

She rolls her eyes. "Dad, swear to god, that woman has problems."

"I'm sure she does, but she's still your teacher, and I'm meeting with her tomorrow. So tell me why she says you're disruptive and disrespectful."

"You call me that all the time," she mutters.

"Cara."

Cue the big, dramatic sigh. "I couldn't keep my mouth shut, Dad. I *was* disrespectful, and I've already apologized for that—though not with enough groveling to make her happy—but I'm not taking the flak for being disruptive. I'm allowed to ask questions in class. They're all directly relevant to the texts we're reading and the topics under discussion. She just doesn't like it when our opinions are different to hers."

It's my turn to sigh. "I need specific details."

"Fine, easy." She pulls a folder closer and flips through until she finds an assessment sheet—a list of criteria, a Y/N column to show if each had been met, and then the assigned grade and comments. "Look at this. My extra-credit paper on *Flowers for Algernon* met every criterion on her list, but she still gave me a C. When I asked her why, when other students who didn't meet all the criteria got higher grades, she told me the criteria formed the basis of the assessment, but she also needed to take into account narrative style. And when I asked if I could make a time for her to show me the problems with my 'narrative style,' she told me to stop being disruptive. That's what she always says when she wants someone to sit down and shut up."

I scan the assessment sheet. This was poorly thought out—when the criteria are pass/fail like this, the whole assignment should be pass/fail. Otherwise, assign specific value to each criterion. But I guess with extra credit, it's all at the teacher's discretion. "Can I see your paper?"

She flips another few pages, then pulls some stapled papers from a pocket. It's been a long—very long—time since I read *Flowers for Algernon*, but it seems like a decent effort, and I don't see any issues with her "narrative style." I'm no English teacher, but her spelling and grammar are good, the sentences are clear and easy to follow, and her thesis is explained and proven.

I hand the tablet back. "And you think she gave you a C because she doesn't like you?"

Cara shakes her head, then stops. "Well, she doesn't like me, but honestly, I don't think that's why I got the C. I think I got the C because my paper disputes one of her favorite theories about the book. I was talking about it with some of the others, and the ones who went with the theses she's always spouting off in class got higher grades on average, even if they didn't meet every criterion."

I rub my forehead, feeling a headache build. "Okay. So you challenged her in class about this today—"

"No, this was last week."

Whoa. "Last week? And you're just going to take the C even though you think you deserve better?" Who is this girl and what has she done with my daughter?

"Don't be dumb, Dad. The C was only one symptom of a bigger problem." Ah. There she is. "Assessing criteria as pass/fail doesn't work in situations like this because it gives the teachers too much room to let bias creep in. The second I say anything about Mrs. Hamilton grading me unfairly, I lose all credibility—"

"How so?" It's my turn to interrupt.

"Because she's given me detention at least once a week since I got here. People are going to say I'm just trying to get back at her."

"Excuse me… at least once a week? Why haven't I heard about this? Shouldn't the school have been in contact if you're in trouble that much?"

She shrugs. "I don't know. It's weird, now that you mention it."

I make a mental note to follow it up while I'm at the school tomorrow. "So what is your plan, then?" Because I know she's got one. She takes after both her parents in that.

"A bunch of us are putting together a proposal for the head of the English department, showing how the current extra-credit assessment system isn't working and how we'd like to see it standardized across the whole department."

Pride bursts in my chest. *That's my girl!*

I clear my throat. "And is the head of the department likely to pay any attention?"

Tipping her head to the side, she purses her lips thoughtfully. "I think so. It's hard for me to judge, because I haven't been taught by him, but the others all say he's cool. Tough grader, but really fair about assignments and always willing to help if you need it." She shrugs again. "But if he doesn't, we take it to the principal. We're not asking for any advantages. If anything, these changes will make it tougher to get extra credit. But it's too hard with the current system to actually learn from mistakes."

I consider that in silence for a moment. "Okay, then, what happened today that caused you to be 'disruptive'?"

I'm expecting another eye roll, but this time Cara gets mad. Her face flushes, and she bangs her hand on the table. "She passed around a list of books we could read for extra credit. I mean, the school has an official one already, but this was another list that she thought we could 'benefit' from."

"And you didn't think any of those books were beneficial?" Cara's always read widely and ahead of her age group. Her mother and I encouraged it, with the caveat that she come to us with any questions she might have. It's spurred a lot of discussions over the years on a wide range of topics.

"No, but that's not the point. I didn't say anything. I swear, Dad, I kept my mouth shut. But I guess I might have made a face or something, because she was all, like, is there a problem? And I said no, because I didn't want to start anything over a list that's not mandatory, but she just wouldn't let it go. She said it seemed like there was a problem and was I sure I didn't want to share anything with the class." She takes a breath. "I just wanted her off my back, so I said there was no problem, but I hadn't enjoyed *Tess of the d'Urbervilles* when I read it."

I cringe. I remember that—she definitely did not enjoy it, and when my ex and I realized she'd read it and what it was about, we weren't thrilled either.

"What did she say then?"

And there's the eye roll. "She said it really wasn't surprising that someone my age was unable to understand Hardy's brilliance and that I should try again and look for the moral in the story." She squeezes her eyes shut. "Dad, I thought that she might mean that I should look at the plot of the book and the type of thinking it embodied as a clear signpost that those times needed to change. And I got so excited about that idea that I asked her which approach she thought I should take, classism or feminism, and she shot me down. Said I'd clearly missed the central theme of the book, which was that societal norms are in place for a reason and people who flout them get their just desserts."

For a moment, I can't see through the red film blocking my vision. She said *that*? About a book where a wealthy young man rapes a village girl, then years later takes advantage of the fact that she and her family are desperate to force her to become his mistress because she has no other options? A book that ends with her execution? My seventeen-year-old daughter was told that *that* is a societal norm she should respect?

Fuck that!

My explosion of wrath is forestalled by the ding of the oven timer. Cara gets up to get dinner, and I take advantage of the break to get myself under control. By the time she brings dinner to the table and I move to the eating side, I can even manage a small smile.

"Thanks, this looks great. You remembered extra cheese."

She snorts. "Like I could forget. You've only been asking for extra cheese all my life."

We dig in, and I wait a few bites before I ask, "So how bad was the explosion?"

Her huff of laughter is reassuring. "Not that bad, really. I said that I disagreed and wasn't interested in extra credit if it meant I had to pretend that *Tess* had any value as a moral compass in the modern world. And that it's long been agreed that Hardy was, in his own classist, misogynistic way, trying to show that the world needed to move forward, but—" She winces. "—uh, but that since she was raised in that world, she might not be able to let go of the past."

It's weird: my stomach has just dropped like a lead balloon, but I still need to clench my teeth to keep from laughing.

"Oh, Cara."

"I know. And I apologized right away. I shouldn't have made personal comments, and I told her that. But she was pissed, so I got detention and she called you."

I eat a few more bites, trying to decide how the hell I'm going to handle this. Telling your teacher she's over a hundred and thirty years old is bad. But that's not the only issue here.

"You deserved that detention," I told her. "You've completely undermined yourself and me. Any leg we had to stand on was knocked away as soon as you made it personal."

"I know," she says glumly.

"You know it doesn't worry me and your mom when you argue with teachers as long as you're respectful and make good, valid, and valuable points. Pointing out that the societal values in *Tess* are no longer valid and that Hardy was trying some form of evangelism was fine. But that last bit…"

"I know," she groans. "I knew while it was coming out of my mouth, but she made me so mad. I just couldn't stop."

"Well, you're grounded until Tuesday. School and work only."

She groans again but doesn't argue.

"Is there anything else I should know before this meeting?"

Her snort doesn't make me feel better. "Lots, probably. But I doubt it'll come up."

Great.

TWO

Oliver

_____

Classes are done for the day, and for once, I don't have any clubs to oversee or meetings to go to. The miracle of having a few hours to spare is due to a combination of an overnight sophomore science camp and a weird run of gastric flu that's taken out some of the staff. Note to self: stay *far* away from the teachers' lounge for a few days.

Regardless of the reason, I've been able to actually clear my inbox and am thinking about heading home to do some grading. If I do it here, eventually someone will stick their head around the office door and ask for something. I rarely grade assignments in my office. There's just too much else to do.

I'm not complaining. It sounds like I am, but honestly, I love it. Not so much the staff meetings, but being a part of shaping young minds—introducing them to amazing worlds and the wonder and versatility of words—that's something I will never get tired of. That's why I volunteer to be the faculty advisor for more school clubs and associations than I really should. That's why I applied for the job of head of the English department when Kelly Green left two years ago. It adds to my workload, but it gives me more input into the curriculum and lets me help more of the kids.

Ugh. I sound like a real nerd, don't I? I mean, I am, but I didn't mean to show it quite this soon.

The phone rings, the line flashing for the front office. And damn, there goes my plan to sneak out early and get a head start on that grading.

"Hi, Maria," I say as cheerfully as I can, considering I don't know what she's going to ask me for.

"Oliver, I'm so sorry, there's a parent on his way to you."

That doesn't sound good. "I don't have any appointments," I tell her, my eyes going to my computer screen, where my calendar is up. No, definitely nothing today.

"He asked for Darryn"—the principal—"but he's already left for that conference, and Mai"—the vice-principal—"is out sick. Then he asked me who he could speak with who had any power over the English department, and your name just slipped out. I'm so sorry."

And of course, it's not difficult to find offices here. Some genius put them all in the administration wing when designing the school. Not always convenient.

"Maybe it's not a bad thing he wants to talk about."

I can almost hear her wince. "He, uh, he just had a meeting with Edith," she whispers, and I groan out loud.

Unprofessional, yes, but totally justified.

"Thanks, Maria. I'll handle it."

She apologizes again before ending the call. I have literally seconds before this parent arrives—unless he's navigationally challenged and managed to get lost walking down a straight corridor—and all I can think is how very glad I will be when Edith Hamilton retires.

Don't get me wrong. She's not a bad teacher. She loves teaching and loves the English language. Loves introducing students to new concepts and ideas through literature.

But she's old-fashioned and very rigid in her thinking. I know she plays favorites with the students—there have been a few complaints, but I can't quite work out how she chooses her favorites. In the past, I've seen teachers who clearly favor girls over boys, or vice versa, or are racist, or classist. I've seen teachers pick favorites based on dress sense and hairstyle. But Edith's favoritism shows no rhyme or reason that I can see without being in her classroom. Regardless, she and I have had words about it—gentle words at first, then a little bit sharper—and I really thought that this year—her last year—would be better.

Guess not.

There's a sharp knock, then the door is opened before I can call out. A tall, dark-haired man in office attire steps in and closes the door behind him. "Are you Mr. Jeffries?"

I stand and come around the desk. That doesn't leave a lot of room—we're both big men, and the office is small—but I want to take control of this meeting before it begins. "Yes, I'm Oliver Jeffries. Is there something I can help you with?"

He thrusts out a hand. "Dominic Hurst. You're the head of the English department?"

I shake his hand, a little surprised. "Ah, yes. I am." In a town like Joyville, which exists solely to support Joy Universe, everyone knows who the JU bigwigs are. After all, they're the people whose decisions will affect our quality of life. When JU does well, the town grows. When the theme parks are having a downturn, people get laid off. They leave Joyville, and the local businesses suffer.

Nobody even wants to think about what would happen if Joy Universe had to close down. Joyville would die.

So, yes, I know who Dominic Hurst is. He's the new —well, relatively new—guy in charge. And it's early days yet, but things seem to be thriving under his command.

I didn't know he had a kid—kids?—at this school, though.

Pulling myself together, I go back around my desk and take my seat, gesturing him to the visitor chair. "Please, sit. What can I do for you today, Mr. Hurst?"

"Dom," he says, and I guess that's an invitation to call him that? "I want to make a complaint."

Of course he does.

"Okay." I'm not saying anything else until I have more information, so I wait.

So does he.

Finally, a faint smile tugs at the corner of his mouth. "I've just come from a meeting with Mrs. Hamilton," he says. "My daughter, Cara, is having some issues in her class."

My fingers twitch. I want so badly to look up Cara's class record and see what the problem might be, but it's best to let him finish first.

"Learning issues or behavioral issues? Or both?"

He tips his head slightly with a thoughtful expression. "I guess you could say both. Cara's a very forthright and determined person, and she and Mrs. Hamilton don't see eye to eye. It seems to be having an impact on her grades—especially her extra-credit work." He extends his left hand, and for the first time, I notice that he's holding some folded paper. Oh, goody. The parent has brought an assignment he thinks should have been graded higher.

I take the papers and unfold them. On top is an assessment sheet—not an official one, but an extra credit assessment put together by Edith. One look tells me what the problem is. Every criterion met, but only a C? Edith's at it again.

Holding in my sigh, I flip to the next page and begin to skim over the assignment. It doesn't take me long to see that there's nothing wrong with the narrative style and that the student—Cara—has just unfortunately taken an angle that Edith strongly dislikes. I know, because it's happened before. I guess it was too much to hope that Edith had gotten over this.

Looking back at Dominic Hurst, I ask, "What is it you'd like from me today?"

"Nothing to do with that, actually." He waves at the paper. "To begin with, I'd like an apology from Mrs. Hamilton," he says bluntly. "I understand that might not happen, but I still plan to make an official complaint. She and Cara had a disagreement about the value of a book yesterday. Cara was rude, inexcusably so, and she's apologized and been given detention. She's also grounded. I'm aware that my daughter clashes with her teachers, and I don't consider rudeness acceptable. She knows that and rarely crosses the line. Mrs. Hamilton requested a meeting with me today. I found her manner abrasive. When I agreed that Cara's comment was unacceptable and explained the steps I'd taken, she informed me that it wasn't sufficient and that she should have expected as much from a man who'd raised someone like Cara."

Whoa. My chest suddenly tight, I stared at him. "She said that?" Not. Good. "Mr. Hurst——"

"Dom," he says curtly.

"Dom, then. I'm so very sorry that a teacher at this school spoke to you that way. Please understand that the school doesn't tolerate that kind of attitude and that I will address this myself." I suck in a breath and look down at the paper I'm still holding. "Uh, it's clear to me that Mrs. Hamilton may have let some bias affect her while grading Cara's assignment. If you'll——"

"No, don't. Cara and some of her classmates are planning to present a proposal to overhaul the grading system for extra-credit assignments. She'll never forgive me if I preempt that."

I sit back, not sure how to take that. "She wouldn't rather have me review her grade anyway?" I check, because since when does a student not want a better grade? Especially when they've gone to the effort of doing an extra-credit assignment.

He shakes his head, that smile peeking out again. "No. I asked her if she wanted me to address this with Mrs. Hamilton, and she said no. She doesn't know I brought that with me—I planned to ask Mrs. Hamilton to walk me through the problems with it, but she never gave me the chance."

I can't help feeling a little niggle of pride that students at this school are showing that level of maturity. Sure, Cara Hurst is a new student, but he said some of her classmates were involved too. I'll definitely do what I can to work with them on this. That kind of initiative and ingenuity needs to be fostered and rewarded.

"I understand. Okay, so I'm going to follow up with Mrs. Hurst and ensure you receive an apology. I'll also discuss it with the principal when he returns from his conference, and she'll likely receive an official reprimand. This school doesn't condone that kind of behavior." I've already said that, but it bears repeating. I can't believe she made that kind of comment. "I'd also like to arrange a meeting with Cara—and you, if you'd like to be present—to discuss her experiences in that class and whether or not she's comfortable remaining there. If she's clashing, as you put it, with Mrs. Hamilton frequently, it may not be a conducive learning environment for her. We can see if her schedule allows for a move to another lit class, or if that's not possible, arrange for some independent learning. But I'd really prefer for her to be involved in that decision."

He nods. "Definitely. She's old enough now to handle that decision herself. I'm not sure she'd agree to independent learning, though. She likes a classroom environment. But you can discuss that with her. I'll check with her tonight if she wants me there, but my guess is no. If there's something she needs me to know, she'll tell me." He hesitates. "In the interest of full disclosure, you should probably know exactly what Cara said that spurred the need for this meeting."

"I'm both afraid and intrigued," I tell him honestly, because this kid sounds like a firecracker.

He winces. "She may have suggested that Mrs. Hamilton was around in the time of Thomas Hardy and found it difficult to let go of her Victorian upbringing."

I bite my lip to hold back laughter. It's an inappropriate comment, of course. Horrifically rude.

Dom Hurst sighs. "Yeah, that was my reaction too. Are we bad people?"

I shake my head, fighting to regain control so that when I open my mouth, a laugh won't come out. "No," I finally manage. "If we were bad people, we would've laughed and not disciplined Cara. She got detention, you said?"

He nods. "And she's grounded."

"Then I think that's been dealt with. If Mrs. Hamilton is still here, I'll have a word with her now, and I'll arrange some time to meet with Cara tomorrow." I'm not sure when, but I'll make it happen. I'm particularly concerned that this problem might not be confined just to her. I knew Edith played favorites, but not to the point of grading an A paper a C. It doesn't matter that it's for extra credit—students deserve the grades they deserve.

"Thank you," he says, standing and holding out his hand again. I get up and shake it, then watch him leave and sink back into my chair. I might try calling Darryn before I hunt down Edith. This is definitely something he needs to know about.

I sigh. So much for getting some grading done.

THREE

Dom
_____

When I get home from work the next night, Cara looks much happier.

"Hey," I say, leaning over to kiss her head. "Good day? Did Mr. Jeffries talk to you?" We had a long debrief when I got back from the school yesterday, trying to decide how she wanted to move forward.

"Yeah, I met with him instead of going to my lit class," she says. "He seems cool, Dad. I really don't think Mrs. Hamilton's class is right for me, so we tried to get me switched to Mr. Lang's class, but we couldn't make it work. Instead, we set it up as independent study with Mr. Lang as my teacher."

"And you're happy with that?" I help myself to a glass of water and peer into the wok on the stove. Stir-fry—and she left out the snow peas. I have the world's best daughter.

"Well, it's not ideal. I prefer a shared learning experience." I bite my lip hard to keep from laughing, because even if she is almost an adult and extremely mature, hearing my little girl who used to burp the alphabet say something as buzzword-y as "shared learning experience" is funny. "But this is a good solution that I'm comfortable with. I don't need to be worrying about Mrs. Hamilton when I should be focused on grades."

"Okay. If you're happy, I'm happy."

"Good. Because while I was talking to Mr. Jeffries, I realized exactly how long it's been since you've been on a date."

Bam. Right out of left field.

I waste a few seconds wondering how she made any of those connections, then give up.

"Excuse me?"

She nods, flashing me her most convincing smile— the one she gets from me. "Seriously, Dad. You haven't dated at all since I got here, and I bet not before then, either."

Sighing, I put down my glass and then cross to sit with her at the table. That's two nights now it's seen us have A Serious Conversation. "I've been a little busy lately, Cara. Finishing up at my old job, moving from Boston, getting settled in at a new company with a lot of pressure to make a difference right away. Then suddenly you were here too, and I'm so glad you are, but it wasn't expected, and I had to make some adjustments."

She tips her head to the side, still smiling. "That's such bullshit."

"Cara! It is not." Except it really, really is. But I don't have to admit that to her.

"It so is. If you really wanted to meet someone, you could. And don't even think about using me as an excuse ever, because I'm a strong proponent of you finding someone and being happy."

"I don't need to find someone to be happy," I say immediately, because that's something her mother and I have tried to instill in her from the moment she was old enough to understand.

"Yeah, but are you happy? Like, really happy? Because all you do is work and hang out with me. I love you, Dad, and I'm really glad I get to spend this time with you, but in about nine months I'm going to be gone, and I don't want you to get lonely. So even if you don't want to date someone, maybe you could try making some new friends?"

I open my mouth and then close it again. Jesus fuck, when did my kid grow up? Seriously.

"I'm not against dating or friends," I say finally. "But work doesn't really leave me a lot of time right now, and I want to spend what I've got with you. I do see your point, though, and I'll make an effort to get out more whenever you're not home."

She spreads her hands. "That's all I'm asking. And hey, why don't we download some dating apps to your phone? That's a great way to meet people."

"I'm covered, thanks," I tell her, then wish I hadn't when her eyes widen.

"*Really?* Like, actual dating apps, or hookup apps?"

"In my head, you don't even know what a hookup is." Oh my god, should I be checking her phone for Tinder or something? My ex and I used to monitor her social media when she was younger, but the last couple years we figured she was old enough and mature enough to come to us if something wasn't right.

She laughs. "Whatever, Dad. Let's pretend I've been living in a convent. Have you used them since you got here?"

Jesus. "Cara, there are a lot of things I'm happy to discuss with you, but whether or not I use hookup apps is not one of them."

"Fine." She rolls her eyes. "What about friends, then? Are there any cool people at work you could hang out with without it being weird?" She's aware that it can be very awkward for me to have friendships in the workplace. When you're the big boss, people tend to be either uncomfortable going out for a beer, or ridiculously ingratiating.

"Maybe," I say, thinking about my exec team. "It's still early days, though, and I don't want anyone to think I'm playing favorites."

"We could have a party," she suggests. "You can invite all the senior people and their partners. They can hang out, eat, drink, and it'll be clear pretty soon who you click with. Then nobody can say you didn't give them a chance to befriend you."

I can't even. "It's not that simple," I begin. "For starters, where would we even have the party? They won't all fit here."

She shrugs. "We'll work something out. Just say you'll think about it. Please?"

"I'll think about it," I dutifully promise. "Now, dinner?"

"Heck, yes." She closes her biology textbook. "I'm starving."

If only she was always this easy to distract.

———

Cara's school schedule picks up after that with a barrage of assignments and afterschool activities, and she seems to have forgotten that she wants me to be more social. On my part, I make a tiny bit more of an effort—when Toby, the head of the events department, invites me to join his team for a celebratory drink after they pull off a big event, I go. It's a little uncomfortable, as several people are very obvious in their efforts not to get stuck talking to the boss, but Toby is very easygoing and manages to smooth over the gaffes. I meet his boyfriend, who works at one of the resorts as a chef, and it's great to see how open and natural they are about their relationship at a company event. One of the companies I worked for earlier in my career was pretty homophobic. Officially, they "welcomed diversity," but the truth was, if you didn't fit within their lines, they found a reason to get rid of you.

Of course I expected JU to be different—after all, the founder was a gay Black man, and the executive team is relatively diverse. But expectations can be tricky, and it's nice that mine have been met.

So, yeah… I've been putting a minimum of effort in on the social thing, and honestly, I've been thinking I should try harder. Cara has an overnight field trip this Friday, and it would be a great opportunity for me to dust the cobwebs off some of those apps. It's been a long time since my dick had more company than just my hand.

I'm in the break room, shaking the last few crumbs from a bag of chips I liberated from the vending machine for my lunch—don't judge me—when two members of the exec team come in, deep in heated discussion.

"I'm just saying, it sounds made up. I really don't want to tell her yes and then find out it was just an excuse so she could sleep over at Jamie's," Luke Durrant, the head of the audit department, says.

"So call his parents on some pretext and find out if they'll be home this weekend. If they will, you'll know it's a real thing," Grant Davis, one of my assistant directors, tells his boyfriend.

Luke shakes his head. "Are you crazy? If Mila finds out I did that, she'd go berserk. I'm glad she's confident that I'm not going to leave, but I don't love the screaming about how I'm horrible and she hates me."

I snort, remembering when Cara was like that. My kid has always been mature, but she is still a teenager.

Grant and Luke turn, seeming to notice me for the first time. "Oh, sorry, Dom. Didn't see you there." Grant heads for the vending machine.

"You've got a daughter, right?" Luke asks. He knows I do, because when Cara first moved down here, I asked him what he thought of Joyville High School.

"Yep," I confirm. "Cara's a senior. And don't worry so much about being a horrible person. She'll grow out of that."

"Soon, I hope," he mutters. "If your daughter who was dating a boy two years older said the school was holding an all-night book reading that she wanted to go to, wouldn't you think she'd made it up to sneak extra time with her boyfriend? During which time they might be doing things I don't want to think about her doing?"

I think about it. "Yeah, I would," I agree, "but in this case, let me set your mind at rest. The English department is holding an all-night reading this Friday. It's a mandatory field trip for the senior English lit classes, but the permission form I had to sign said it's open to other students—and that parents are welcome."

"Really?" Grant turns around. "An all-night reading? I remember they had those at college, though I never went. Lit was never my thing."

"I went to one once," Luke says, still looking surprised. "My roommate was an English major and didn't want to go alone. So this is actually a school event?"

I nod. "Supervised by teachers and everything. You'll have to sign a permission form if she wants to be there."

"Oh." He blinks a few times. "I guess I should let her go, then."

He still sounds reluctant, and a little voice that sounds suspiciously like Cara nudges me. "Why don't we all go for a bit? You can check it out, make sure you're comfortable, and then we can get dinner. Or, wait, you've got another kid, don't you?"

"He's got a baseball camp this weekend," Grant says. "Would your daughter mind you being there? Because Mila would freak out if we turned up on our own, but if we make it a group event, she'd be okay."

"Cherish the freak-out," I tell him. "Cara used to do that, but now she takes pleasure in finding ways to embarrass me. I can guarantee that if I'm there, she'll make me take a turn reading and insist I do voices or something. Or she'll try to set me up with one of the other parents."

Luke laughs. "I would pay actual money to see you reading with voices, so we are definitely coming."

"I feel as though I may have just made a mistake," I joke.

Grant tosses a candy bar to Luke and raises a brow at me. "Want anything?"

I hold up my empty chip packet. "This was my second. I'd rather not get yelled at when I go for my mandated physical."

He snorts and turns back to get his own bag of chips, then joins me and Luke leaning against the counter. "So, your daughter—Cara, right?" I nod. "Cara's trying to hook you up?"

I roll my eyes and sigh. "She's worried I'll get lonely when she goes to college." I look at Luke. "Be thankful you're not single anymore, or you'd have to sit through having your kid ask you if you use hookup apps."

Grant chokes on his chips. "Oh my god," he wheezes. "She didn't!" Luke pounds on his back while he coughs and sputters.

"Please don't die on company premises," I say dryly. "The paperwork would be a bitch."

That starts him choking again, this time with laughter, while Luke chuckles helplessly beside him. A lot of people wouldn't get it, but I can guarantee that at exec level, paperwork is the second thing someone thinks of at a time like this—right after "don't die at all."

When Grant finally wipes his eyes and blows out an exhausted breath, he looks at me and says, "I'm going to take video of you reading and post it on the company app."

"All phones must be turned off for the night," I tell him. Thank fuck. Cara would probably post that shit on social media. "It was on the info sheet. Along with a number to contact in case of emergencies. I'm surprised Mila didn't give it to you already."

"I'm still going to enjoy the crap out of it," Grant insists. "*And* I'm going to tell Cara that you've been saying you want to meet someone. I'll say it *loud*. Just see how fast word gets around—you'll have single moms lining up down your block."

"Just the moms?" This is it: my coming-out-at-work moment. It's not a secret that I'm bisexual, but because I was married to a woman, it never seems to be information that gets around. And sometimes, even when it does, people act like it can't be true because I was married to a woman. Bi erasure is so much more common than people think.

Luke shrugs. "If you want the dads too, Grant's gonna need to make some more loud comments so everyone knows." He looks thoughtful. "Although if you seriously are looking for—"

"No."

"But—"

"No." Oh, hell no. I've seen how fast gossip flies around this place. I've heard all about the betting pools. I *do not* need people at work getting involved with my love life.

Of course, I'd have to have one first. But that's not happening through work. No fucking way.

"Fine," Luke concedes. "We'll let Cara handle it."

Grant just grins evilly.

THAT NIGHT OVER DINNER, I ask Cara if she's okay with me coming to the reading.

"Sure." She sounds surprised. "It'll be fun. Uh, any particular reason you want to come?"

"I'm actually going to meet up with some people from work and go out after," I tell her. "They've got a kid at your school—younger than you, though. Mila Durrant?"

Her brow furrows, and she shakes her head. "I don't know a Mila Durrant. But it's a big school. Wait, do you mean Mila Marks? She's dating a guy who was in Mrs. Hamilton's class with me."

I shrug. "That might be it. I'm not exactly sure what her surname is." I've worked close enough with Luke to know his kids are actually his niece and nephew.

"It's probably her. Her uncle was the interim director at JU before you got here. I don't know her well, but she seems nice, and Jamie, her boyfriend, is good people. He's in a few of my classes." She clears her throat and puts down her fork. "So, listen, don't get mad, but I haven't told anybody at school who you are."

I put my fork down too. "I'm not mad. What do you mean, who I am? That you live with your dad?"

She rolls her eyes. "No, Dad, jeez. I haven't told them that you're 'the director.'" She makes air quotes and says it in a deep voice, and I bite the inside of my cheek to keep from laughing. "At first it just didn't come up—I said you worked at JU, and nobody asked exactly what you did. Then I started to realize exactly how important JU is around here. Like… this town wouldn't *exist* if it wasn't for JU. Everybody knows who's on the exec team and what they're doing. I heard some of the bitchy girls talking about Mila, saying how she's not so hot now that her uncle isn't in charge anymore—"

"Are people picking on her?" I ask sharply, because I know Luke would want to do something about that.

Cara huffs and shakes her head. "No. Like I wouldn't have already done something if they were. She and Jamie are popular enough that nobody would say anything to her face, anyway. But my point is, I don't want to be the girl people are nice to because my dad's the one in charge. Some of the kids who don't like me now, who tell me I should just shut up, I've seen the way they suck up to kids whose parents have senior jobs at JU. I don't want to deal with the fakeness of it all. And if someone gets fired for whatever good reason I'm sure you'd have, I don't want to deal with the fallout from their kids at school. I just want to get through this year like a normal teenager."

There're a few moments of silence while I turn that over. "I know this isn't your point, but are kids really telling you to shut up?" I hate the thought of her being bullied.

She sighs. "Yeah, sometimes. But it's always been that way. When you speak up, there's always someone who wants to silence you. It's not bad—I don't feel unsafe or anything. Usually I just tell them to fuck off."

I ignore the cursing. Her mom hates it, but I know she doesn't do it indiscriminately, and she's nearly an adult. "But you'll tell me if it gets to the point where you're uncomfortable?"

"Yeah, Dad." She nods. "I promise."

"Okay. Well, I'm not mad. I get where you're coming from, and I'm genuinely sorry that my job has put you in this position. Has it always been this way?" God, has my daughter been struggling through school because of my work?

"Nah. When we were in Boston, and even in Chicago, there were so many kids whose parents had senior jobs at different companies that nobody cared. It's really just because here, Joy Universe is everything, you know?"

"I know." It was actually kind of daunting when I first realized how much the town depended on the complex. "I'll have a word with Luke and Grant and make sure they don't mention it. My name might be a problem, though," I point out. "If you want, I don't have to come on Friday."

She shakes her head. "Just introduce yourself as my dad. Hurst is a common enough surname that nobody's put it together yet. Don't wear a suit, and maybe smile, and then you won't look like the picture on the website."

I blink. "Smile?"

"Yeah." She makes a face. "No offense, Dad, but you look kind of robotic in all your publicity pictures. Super serious and like you never have any fun."

"I do not!" Do I? It actually might be possible. I try to look professional and businesslike for those things— I'm the company director, for fuck's sake. People need to know that I take that seriously, not wonder if I'm planning to take the afternoon off and go to the beach.

"Yeah, you do. It's okay, though. I love you anyway. And it works out for the best, because if you come dressed casual and smiling like a normal person, nobody will recognize you."

That seems like wishful thinking to me, but I'm not going to argue. "Okay, sure. I'll make sure I smile."

"So you're making friends at work? That's really great, Dad. I'm so proud of you."

Kill me now.

FOUR

Oliver

The gym is a mass of chattering, excited students with sleeping bags and the occasional parent. We've had a better turnout than I expected, considering this is the first time we've ever done this. The students in the senior lit classes are all here, checked off the attendance register, and there's a surprising number of other students, both seniors and younger. It's possible they think this is going to be a good opportunity to stuff around and make out—in which case, they will be sorely disappointed—but I prefer to believe they genuinely want to take part in our all-night reading of Lynn Flewelling's *Luck in the Shadows*.

The students picked the book, by the way, from a list they were given. This is a field trip with an assignment due at the end of next week on the differences between literary and popular fiction, citing this book vs any of the texts on their recommended reading list. Usually we allow the students to select both books and do the assignment individually, but this year I decided it would be a good idea to try something different. Most of the teachers involved are enthusiastic about the idea, but Edith said it was ridiculous and declined to supervise. I didn't argue. She's never liked this particular assignment anyway, since she has opinions about popular fiction that belong in... well, to reference Cara Hurst's views, Victorian times.

Speaking of Cara Hurst, I saw her come in not long ago with her dad. I was surprised to see him—he didn't strike me as the kind who felt the need to supervise his kid on an accompanied field trip, and after talking with Cara for five minutes, I got the decided impression that she wouldn't tolerate it if he was. She's one independent and determined teenager. I have an appointment with her and some others next week to discuss "issues with unconscious bias in the extra-credit assessment system." Thanks to her dad's tip, I know what to expect and am prepared to negotiate.

I'm actually looking forward to it. Having a standardized assessment model for extra-credit assignments would probably be a good thing and make things easier for staff.

For now, though... I look around the room, catch sight of Dominic Hurst standing with two other men I don't recognize, and head that way.

"...so apparently I need to smile more," he's saying, and both the other men are laughing.

"Excuse me," I say, and they all turn to me. "Please forgive the interruption."

"Not at all," Dom—he did say I could call him that —assures me. "Luke, Grant, this is Oliver Jeffries, the head of the English department."

I shake hands with both of them. "It's great to meet you," one says. "I'm Luke Durrant—my niece, Mila, is in one of your classes. She's a sophomore."

I smile, because Mila's a great student. "I'm so glad Mila came tonight. I look forward to seeing you at parent-teacher conference time—I have a lot of good things to say."

His grin is instant. "You have no idea how glad I am to hear that. This is my boyfriend, Grant Davis."

"Good to meet you. I'm kind of sorry we're not staying all night," Grant admits. "I read this book when I was in college and really liked it."

That's music to my ears, of course. "If you like, I'd be happy to give you a copy of the popular fiction recommended reading list we have for the students. I love to encourage families to read together." The intro-duction told me more than their names, of course—like I've said before, everyone knows who's at the top at JU, and Luke Durrant was the interim director for several months earlier this year. Grant's been an assistant director for nearly two years.

"That sounds great," he replies, sounding a little surprised but pleased.

"I'll have it when you come to pick Mila up," I promise, wishing I'd thought to bring them with me. I turn to Dom. "Uh, could I have a quick word?"

"Of course."

"We'll just go see where the kids want us to sit," Luke says. "I'm not sure if Mila likes us enough tonight to sit with us or not."

I choke down the urge to laugh as they walk away. It's not the first time I've heard a parent say something like that, and it makes me thankful that I get to give the kids back at the end of the school day, especially when they've been very challenging in class.

"What can I do for you?" Dom asks. "Oh—before I forget, I'm just Cara's dad tonight. She'd prefer if…" He hesitates, clearly not sure how to finish.

"I understand," I assure him. "It can be tough enough being a teenager without having a 'famous' parent."

He snorts. "All those people trying to break into the entertainment industry to be famous, and who knew all you had to do was move to a town dependent on a theme park complex?"

"You make it sound so easy," I say dryly. "Don't be so modest. Not everyone could do your job."

There's a particularly loud shout from across the gym, and he winces. "I could say the same to you. Not many people would volunteer to spend their Friday night with nearly a hundred teenagers." His eyes lock with mine, and for a second, I feel breathless and hot. It's not often I get complimented by an attractive, intelligent, powerful man. Who's younger than me, to boot.

I drag my gaze away and force myself to ignore the slight stirring of interest in my pants. It's clearly been too long since I had sex—what is it now? A year? A little more, I think.

"Uh, thank you. They'll have fun tonight, and that will encourage them to associate reading with a good time, and…" I shrug. "That's the whole point, right? Uh, anyway, I just wanted to make sure you're happy with the way things were resolved for Cara. Do you have any further concerns?" Time to put my professional hat on.

He shakes his head. "Cara seems satisfied. I know

she would have preferred to be in a class and not doing independent study, but since it couldn't be done, she'd rather not give up lit entirely. And I received an apology email from Mrs. Hamilton, so as far as I'm concerned, the matter is done."

I hold in my sigh of relief. "Good. Thank you. Again, I'm so sorry for—"

He holds up a hand, smiling. "No need. It's done, and I'm happy with the way the school and you handled the matter."

I nod. "Great. Well, I guess I'd better get things started here. Are you planning to stay long? And will you be reading?"

He groans. "According to Cara, I will definitely be reading. We'll stay for an hour or so, I guess."

"I'll make sure you get a chance to read before you go, then," I assure him with a grin, then head toward the middle of the room to get everyone's attention, basking in the warm sound of his laughter behind me.

I STAY true to my word, but even if I hadn't, Cara would have made sure her dad had a turn reading. I know this because she announced it as we all settled down, a book for every two or three people.

"My dad needs to take a turn reading before he goes," she declared to everyone. "It's my revenge for him grounding me the other week."

The students all hooted and hollered, while parents moaned and chuckled in sympathy, and Dom sighed, laughingly shook his head, and agreed.

"Does anybody object if Cara's dad goes first?" I ask, being careful not to use his name. Nobody seems to care, so I continue, "Remember, there's no obligation for anyone to read, although if there are no volunteers at all, you'll have to listen to me droning on all night." A chuckle goes around the room. "If you do decide to read, it can be as little as you like, but no more than a scene at a time—let's make sure everyone who wants a turn gets it. You can always read more than once. And finally—and I'm only going to say this once; there will be no warnings—be respectful of whoever is reading. No talking. We'll be stopping occasionally for discussion, but you can always raise your hand if you have a question. And I'm sure I don't need to remind you that we have a zero-tolerance policy toward bullying. Anybody who makes fun of anyone else will face consequences per our anti-bullying policy. Understood?"

There's a general murmur of agreement. I'm not stupid enough to think we don't have bullies at the school, but I doubt we'll have any problems tonight. Most of the lit students have brought paper along for taking notes as we read, and the others voluntarily came to an all-night reading. Hopefully they'll be more interested in the book than anything else.

I give Dom a nod, and he begins to read. He's got a great voice, deep, but not so much that it's hard for the ear to catch individual words, and he speaks at an even, steady pace, enunciating clearly but not overly. He's obviously had training in public speaking, and if he ever finds himself needing a new career, he could give audiobook narration a shot and have some decent success.

And then he gets to the first bit of dialogue and

shocks us all with a high-pitched falsetto. An explosion of surprised laughter echoes through the room. He grins and waits us out, then continues, maintaining the voice perfectly and with just the right intonation on certain words.

After the first five pages, multiple character voices, and an accidental s-bomb when he realizes he's mixed two of them up, he pauses and says, "That's it for me. Anyone else want a turn?"

There's a moment of hesitation, then one of the students says, "I'll go," and starts reading—not quite as smoothly, but well enough for everyone to follow. I catch Dom's gaze and give him a grateful smile—nobody ever wants to be the first reader, so I was pretty sure I'd have to start—and he smiles back.

And I get that breathless feeling again.

Uh-oh.

I really thought I was past getting crushes. I'm fifty-six years old. I had my kind-of wild youth—well, okay, it wasn't wild at all. My idea of a crazy time in college was one of these all-night readings or passing around a bong and some cheap bourbon with a few friends while we debated all sorts of pretentious shit like we actually knew what we were talking about. But regardless, I had my fair share of indiscriminate sex. I've crushed wildly on people who were never going to crush back, including more than one straight guy. I've been in relationships, very short and pretty long and somewhere in between. Over time, my sex drive has settled down into something a little more comfortable. There isn't that excited *push* for sex that I used to have, just a kind of "sex would be nice" feeling that I can take or leave, depending on whether I'm in the mood. It ramps up a little more when I'm seeing someone—or crushing on someone. Which, like I said, I thought I was past.

Except that's clearly not the case, because just looking at Dominic Hurst's smile is causing a rush of butterflies in my stomach.

FIVE

Dom

We leave the school at the first bathroom break, just under two hours after reading began. Honestly, I wouldn't have minded hanging around—it was more fun than I thought it would be, even if some of the parents now hate me for accidentally swearing in front of their kids. Is "shit" even a real swear word, though? And these are high school kids—they've definitely heard worse, even if they haven't said it themselves. Not all parents agree, though, and I got quite a few disapproving glares.

Anyway, Cara might not have cared that I came, but she probably would have if I'd stayed all night, so when Luke asked if I was ready to go, I agreed. He seems much more comfortable now with the idea of Mila being there, especially after she took a turn reading and seemed to really enjoy it.

As we stroll toward our cars, idly discussing where to go eat, Grant checks his phone. "Dom, do you mind if Derek joins us? He's bored and hungry."

Derek Bryer is one of the other assistant directors at

JU. I know he and Grant are close, and he was one of the other people on the shortlist of possible friends that I mentally created when Cara was nagging me about it.

"Sure. As long as he likes burgers, because I have a craving now."

Grant snorts, texting back. "Don't worry, he'll definitely go for a burger. They try to eat healthy as much as possible at home because Trav needs to keep in shape, so this will be his chance to go nuts."

If I'm remembering the office gossip—which Layla keeps me up to date with—Trav is Derek's boyfriend, a performer for the Joy Village Theater Company. Who, since it's a Friday night, is no doubt working.

"Sounds good to me," I assure them, pausing as we reach my car. "I'll see you there." They wave, and I get in the car feeling pretty damn good. It's nice not to be home alone watching crap TV on a Friday night. I mean, I foresee wanting to spend many Friday nights that way in the future, because work can be brain-destroying and sometimes I only want to switch off with takeout and a beer, but after spending so many months with only my own company and Cara's, I'm really looking forward to some time with other people.

I start the car. This will be good.

I'M LAUGHING my ass off at one of Derek's work stories —he's been at JU longer than any of the rest of us and he has a stockpile of gossip and funny anecdotes—when our server comes around and clears some of the empty plates.

"Can I get you guys some more drinks?" he asks,

smiling flirtatiously. He's a cute, friendly kid and clearly knows how to work customers for better tips. I used to do the same when I was working my way through college, though I didn't have his adorable twink factor.

I glance around the table and get nods and yeses. "That sounds great, Cole. Thanks."

He winks. "My pleasure."

As he walks away, Luke snickers. "How do you think Cara would feel about you dating him? Would she still be shit-hot to set you up with someone nearly her own age?"

I roll my eyes. "Fuck, I might mention it just to shut her up. She brought it up again the other day."

"Cara's your daughter?" Derek asks, and when I nod, he adds, "It could be worse. She could never want to let you out of her sight."

I snort. "You've clearly never met Cara."

"Sounds like you need to just go on a date and make her happy. If you do it once, she'll know that you're capable of doing it again."

I throw a balled-up napkin at his head. "She already knows that. I was married to her mother for fifteen years, and I've had a boyfriend since the divorce."

Derek's eyebrows go up. "You swing both ways, huh? That gives us more options."

"No." I point at him. "Absolutely not. I've already said this to Luke, and I'm going to keep saying it as often as I need to. I do not want your help, interference, or interest in my love life."

"Too late for the last one," Grant says cheerfully. "Luke and I were talking about it in the car."

I groan. How could I have forgotten that the downside of having friends is that they take an interest in your life?

"What were you talking about? There's nothing to talk about," I protest, but Derek just talks over me.

"Anything I should know?"

"No!" Seriously, where's the fear of the boss when you need it?

Luke looks me in the eye. "I thought I saw something between you and that Oliver guy—the head of the English department."

I open my mouth to rebut, then close it again.

Because I can't deny a tiny spark of interest at the thought.

"Oooh!" Grant exclaims in delight, grinning widely. "Do you suddenly want us to keep talking?"

"Shut up," I mutter. "It's… He's Cara's teacher." And fuck me, that is so not what I intended to say.

Derek winces. "Yeah, I can see how that would be awkward. Plus, the school might have a policy against it while she's in his class."

I hesitate. "She's not actually in his class."

Grant crows triumphantly, and I look for something to throw at him. Fortunately (for Grant), Cole comes back right then with our drinks, and I take a long gulp of beer instead.

My reprieve doesn't last long, though. As soon as Cole is gone, Derek leans forward. "So is this guy someone we might be interested in?"

"*We* are not interested in anyone. If there any interest, it will be mine alone." Also not what I planned to say. Maybe I should stop drinking. A few beers usually don't affect me, but tonight seems to be the exception.

"And his, of course. You'd definitely need his interest," Luke says, then wiggles his brows like he's got a secret.

I only manage to hold out for a few seconds before I growl, "Fine. And what makes you think he might be interested?"

Luke shrugs. "The fact that he spent more time looking at you than the book, maybe?"

"Tell me about him," Derek demands. "Did you say he's the head of the English department?"

I groan again and thud my head down on the table. I am literally the most powerful person in this town, and I can do nothing to stop this.

"Yeah. Mila's in one of his classes, and she loves him. Older than us—and I think older than Dom," Luke adds, glancing at me, because they're all younger than I am, "maybe around Jase's age. About five ten, medium build, mostly gray, very cool professor beard."

A laugh bursts from me. "What the hell is a professor beard?"

He makes a vague gesture toward his face. "You know. A beard that looks professor-ish."

Grant leans over and kisses his cheek. "It's okay, babe, I know what you mean. But maybe you shouldn't ever pursue a career in creative writing."

"*Anyway*," Luke insists, "he was nice and seems to be really passionate about his job, *and* he couldn't stop staring at Dom. I'm good with vibes, and you two definitely had one."

"I don't know that you're *that* good with vibes," Derek says thoughtfully. "It took you a while to pick up on the one between you and Grant."

"I was trying to be professional," Luke huffs. "And I'm very good with vibes, fuck you very much. I got a vibe that Dom isn't actually straight, and that turned out to be a hundred percent right."

I raise an eyebrow, momentarily distracted. "Really? I thought I was pretty good at keeping all nonwork stuff locked down at the office."

He jabs a finger in my direction. "See! That's how good I am at vibes."

"We're getting off topic," Grant says, shooting that evil grin my way again. "I may not have been able to record Dom reading a book with character voices and saying 'shit' in a room full of teenagers, but there's nothing stopping me from tormenting him about his professor crush."

I scrub my hands over my face. "One, he's not a professor, two, I don't have a crush, and three, I can and will make your life absolute hell. Just so you know."

He just smirks, the bastard, and that's how I know I now actually have friends here. It would feel really good if not for the fact they're tormenting me.

"All jokes aside," Derek interrupts, "is he someone you could be interested in? Because he sounds like a good guy, and it couldn't hurt for you to ask him out for a beer or something."

Sighing, I think about it. I can't deny that if I was going to date anyone right now, Oliver Jeffries would be at the top of my list. His obvious dedication to his students, his enthusiasm for books, and yeah, that whole professor vibe are hugely attractive to me. I like that he's just a little soft around the middle, that he wears sweater vests, and that his hair and beard aren't dyed or overly styled. He's clean and neat but doesn't feel the need to do more—he's comfortable with who he is. I really like that kind of confidence. I'm not a man who lacks self-esteem, and the people I get along best with can stand their ground against my ego.

"Yeah," I concede. "But it's something I'd want to make sure Cara's okay with, since he teaches at her school. I know she's got less than a year left, but…" I shrug.

Grant and Luke shudder in unison. "Can you imagine what Mila would say if I started dating a teacher at her school?" Luke asks, eyes wide with horror.

"Cara's past that stage," I remind them, "but it still might be tricky for her." I shake my head. "It's something to think about, anyway." And honestly, am I in a place to actually date someone? A hookup would be great, because I'm really starting to miss sex with another person, but do I have the time and energy to put into a relationship right now? It's only been a few months since I took over at JU, and the company is in a state of upheaval right now, thanks to the efforts of Luke and his audit team. It would be a lot even if I wasn't new in the job. Plus, Cara's going to be gone in less than a year—wouldn't it be better to concentrate on her right now than find the emotional energy for a new relationship?

So I smile and nod along with the jokes, but I've pretty much made up my mind. I might blow the cobwebs off some of my hookup apps, but dating isn't on my list of priorities right now.

Even if thinking of Oliver that way really gets my motor running.

SIX

Oliver

────────────

I wave off the last of the students and turn to help finish cleaning up. Jaiden Lang, the next-most senior faculty member at the event and my closest friend here in Joyville, ties off a garbage bag and says, "So now that we're alone, I have questions."

I look around the gym, and sure enough, it's empty. "Where did Kate and Emily go?" There had been four of us from the English department on duty last night, as well as several parent volunteers.

Jaiden waves a hand. "I told them to head home. There's not that much left to do... in fact, I think once we haul these to the dumpster, we're done."

A glance proves he's right. The students put away the gym mats that had gone under their sleeping bags before we fed them a breakfast of muffins, fruit, and juice; I've already taken the books back to my office; and there really isn't that much trash left after an all-night reading. It's not like a dance.

"Okay, well let's get on with it, then. I'm exhausted.

I seem to remember it being a lot easier to stay up all night when I was in my twenties."

Snorting, Jaiden passes me a trash bag and hefts the other one, then glances around one more time as though to make sure he hasn't forgotten anything. We leave the gym, pausing for me to lock it, then begin the trek through the school to the exterior door closest to the dumpsters.

"So, are you just going to keep ignoring my rampant curiosity?" he asks.

I roll my eyes. "No, of course not. I wouldn't dream of it. Your rampant curiosity about what?" With Jaiden, it could be anything. Last week we had a forty-five-minute conversation about the best way to collectively refer to species other than human without having humans as the baseline. Spoiler alert: we couldn't think of one. Our conclusion was that humanity is completely human-centric.

"About the hottie you were staring at like he was steak and you were starving."

Heat races up my face, and I've never been more grateful in my life for my beard. It might hide at least some of the blush from him. Because of course I know exactly what he's talking about. I was just hoping I hadn't been quite that obvious.

"I don't know what you mean," I say, trying to sound both confused and amused, like I think he's maybe delusional from lack of sleep.

"Oh, please. Remember who you're talking to. You could barely focus on the book, you were so enthralled by him."

"He's an excellent narrator," I excuse, and instantly know it was a mistake.

"So you do know who I'm talking about, then."

Is it wrong to want to punch your best friend in the face? Yes? Really? It wouldn't be a *hard* punch, just enough to knock that smug tone out of him.

"No, I just—" He gives me a disbelieving look, and I sigh. "Fine. Yes, I know who you're talking about. But I wasn't staring at him like he's steak, for crying out loud. Could you have come up with a more offensive way to describe it?"

He grins, and I stop dead and point at him. "That was *not* an invitation to try, Jaiden."

It's his turn to roll his eyes as we start walking again. "You were staring at him like you wanted to eat him," he insists. "And I saw you talking to him before we got started. Know him well, do you?"

We reach the exterior door, and I pause to punch in the code to disarm the lock and alarm, then reenter it from the outside once we pass through. From here, we can easily walk around to the staff parking lot—there's no need to go back inside the school.

"I don't 'know' him at all," I say, heaving my trash bag into the dumpster. Jaiden follows suit, then closes the lid. "He's Cara Hurst's father. I met with him during that drama with Edith, remember?"

"I know he's Cara's dad, she made that pretty clear. I could have sworn I know him from somewhere, though. I'll have to think about it."

Uh-oh. I glance around, but of course we're alone. "Okay, you can't tell anyone this," I warn him. "Cara doesn't want it becoming general knowledge."

His eyes widen, and he leans in. Secrets and gossip are prime currency around here. "On my grave," he swears, and I chuckle. I never have to worry about being the biggest dork in the group when Jaiden's around.

"He's Dominic Hurst. That's why he looks familiar."

"Domin— Wait, you mean he's the *director*? Oh my god, you're right! He looks different when he's not wearing a suit." He pauses. "Oh, poor Cara. Yeah, better if nobody knows about this." He grabs my arm. "Wait, you're mooning like a lovesick calf over the director?"

Really, would just one punch be so bad? I glare at him, yanking my arm free. "So now I'm the farm animal? A minute ago you said I wanted to eat him. Wouldn't that be cannibalism?"

"Not for the kind of eating I'm thinking of," he mutters salaciously, then waggles his eyebrows when I shoot him an incredulous look. "Oh, come on. He's a very good-looking guy, charismatic, and after hearing him read, I was ready to slip him my number—that was before I realized you were interested, of course. And before I knew he was Cara's dad. She's technically my student, so any nasty business between me and her dad has to wait until she's not."

"Nasty business? Really?" My footsteps are a little on the heavy side as we head toward the staff lot. You might even say I'm stomping. I make a concerted effort not to.

"Oliver, relax, would you? I'd never move on a guy I know you're into. And anyway, have you forgotten about my long-term and long-suffering honey who I'd never cheat on? I'm just teasing you. You're normally not this sensitive."

I mentally slap myself, because he's right—on all counts. Sighing heavily, I bump his shoulder with mine.

"Sorry. I guess I feel a bit weird about this. I thought I was past the age of crushes."

"Buddy," Jaiden begins, slinging an arm around my shoulders, "why is a crush something to feel weird about? If you're past the age of crushing on an attractive man, then what else is there to live for?"

I open my mouth to reply, then stop, because he's kind of right. If you no longer feel that kind of excitement in life, whether it be over a person or a TV show or book or event, then life would be pretty dull. "I still feel weird about it," I finally say, coming to a stop beside my car. "I've never been interested in a parent before. Well, not a parent of a student where I was teaching," I correct. "And like you said, he's the director."

"So?" Jaiden shrugs. "He's still a human being who fucks. Proof of that is his daughter. And further proof of his humanity is that he seems to be a good father. Stood up for his kid. Came last night and let her force him to take the first turn reading. Cara's not the shy, retiring type—half the school knows that she decided to come here and live with her dad for her last year of high school. He's got the money to have sent her to a fancy boarding school, but instead, he added sole custody to what I'm sure is a busy schedule."

"It's not like she needs full-time care. She's nearly an adult," I argue half-heartedly, more because I hate for him to be right too many times in one conversation than for any other reason. He knows it, too, because he pinches me.

"I'm just saying, it's been a while since you dated anyone, and you've obviously got a thing for this guy, so maybe he'd be a good option."

I wince. "Look, yeah, you're not wrong, but I'm not

going to trawl through Cara's file for her dad's phone number so I can call and ask him out. It just doesn't feel right to me."

He huffs a little, then says, "Okay, I get it. I probably wouldn't either. We're just going to have to hope you run into him somewhere. Maybe we can hold another reading or something."

I laugh and unlock the car. "Seriously, you want to plan an event for the students just on the off chance that he might turn up? And then what? I ignore the fact that we're surrounded by a roomful of teenagers, including his daughter, to ask him out? At a school event?"

Jaiden rubs his cheek. "That wouldn't look too good, would it? Leave it with me, though. I'll think of something."

Waving him off, still chuckling, I get in the car and start it. He might be convinced he can find a way to make this work, but I'm okay with the fact that it won't. Some crushes are meant to naturally fade away.

ANYONE WHO SAYS BEING a teacher is easy has no idea what they're talking about. *But look at the hours*, they say, and then bang on about summer vacation and other crap like that. They have no idea how many extra hours teachers put in when students aren't even around. And I can't speak for every teacher, but I know a lot of us have summer jobs once the school year is over. I teach creative writing at the Joyville summer day camp program and tutor high school and college students who want to get ahead before the school year begins.

This week in particular has been agonizing. Everything that could possibly have gone wrong has. Maybe Mercury is in retrograde or something, because the students have been total monsters all week, and it's caused every teacher at the school to seriously reconsider their career path.

But it's finally Friday night, I'm finally done with everything on my to-do list for the week, and I'm finally out of that cursed school. It's nearly six thirty, and I honestly can't stand the idea of cooking tonight, so I'm standing in line at the takeout counter at the best pizza place in town. The best also means the busiest, of course, but I'm willing to wait for what I know will be utter deliciousness. I can take it home, sprawl on the couch in my underwear, and watch something comforting and familiar that I've seen a thousand times until my brain finally shuts off. *Poldark*, maybe, just so I can stare at Aiden Turner in period costume until I feel better.

"Oh, hey."

I wonder if I still have any ice cream in the freezer? I've been trying not to buy it lately, because it's getting harder and harder to keep the extra pounds off, but if any night is an ice-cream nigh—

A hand lands on my arm, and I jump.

"Sorry, I didn't mean to scare you. It just seemed like you didn't hear me."

I know before I turn who I'm going to see, and I can't deny the tingle of excited anticipation that races through me. It's been two weeks since the reading, and I've thought about him a lot.

"Hi. Yeah, I was kind of in an end-of-week daze." I chuckle self-deprecatingly and am relieved that I sound so casual and relaxed. "Here to grab dinner for you and

Cara?" *Groan.* Why else would he be here? I'm such an idiot.

He smiles, those incredible blue eyes twinkling, and I swear, birds sing like we're in a freaking Joy Inc. movie. "Just for me. Cara's going to the football game and then staying with a friend tonight, so I get to spend the evening with my friends: pizza, beer, and Netflix."

"Sounds amazing. That's pretty much my plan too, although I was just thinking about adding ice cream to the mix."

"You have good thoughts." He tips his head and studies me, and then says, "Since our plans coincide so well, why don't we merge them?"

The breath stutters in my lungs. Is he suggesting…?

"Come over to my place. Like I said, Cara won't be home, and I know we have ice cream."

Yes. Yes, he is.

Oh my god.

Wait… is this what I hope it is? Or is he literally just suggesting we not do the exact same thing in two different houses?

Who cares?

"That sounds good," I say, and my voice is even and everything. I'm so busy congratulating myself on it that I almost miss the cashier asking if she can help me.

"Uh…" I look at Dom. "I normally get meatlovers, but—"

"Sounds good," he agrees. "And wings?"

He may just be the perfect man. We order, and there's a brief, awkward scuffle when it's time to pay, which I break by reminding him that he's supplying the ice cream and beer. He reluctantly agrees and puts his credit card away.

There's really no need for us both to wait for the food, but we do, leaning against the wall side by side, chatting about nothing in particular. I didn't expect that it would be so easy to talk to him—I was sure I'd be nervous or say something stupid, as one is wont to do when crushing—but from the moment he mentions the book he's just started reading, I relax and fall into the conversation. I can talk books all day long.

Our number is called before I know it, and as we walk out of the restaurant, we've moved on from biographies to books that have been translated to the screen, and of course I can't resist mentioning *Poldark*. I was just thinking about it earlier, after all.

"I've never watched it," he says, "although I've seen it while I was browsing. I'm not usually into period stuff." We're standing next to my car now, holding our food but not quite ready to separate for even the few minutes it will take to get to his place. It's both ridiculous and thrilling, and I can't believe I ever let myself think that a crush was stupid, no matter my age. How can this delicious feeling be anything but a good thing?

"I'll trade you an episode of *Poldark* for anything you want to watch," I bargain, and he grins.

"Anything? Even if it's some trashy reality show?"

There's a moment of panicky doubt before I think to ask, "Do you watch trashy reality shows?"

He laughs and shakes his head. "No, but I will admit to having a secret addiction to telenovelas."

Oh my god. "You're not going to believe this, but I literally taught myself to speak Spanish by watching telenovelas. I mean, I'm not that great at it, but at least now I can actually follow whose secret daughter is plotting to murder the man she thinks embezzled her stepbrother's illicit fortune but is actually innocent. Before, I was just guessing and making up the plot as I went." And oh fuck, I didn't actually mean to tell him all that, but he's laughing in a "You're so cute and funny way" rather than a "Who is this nutjob and how can I get away" way, so it must be all good.

"I'm parked just over there," he says, pointing. "Follow me home?" I nod, and he flashes me that smile again, the one that makes me so sure tonight isn't just about keeping each other company. I watch for a moment as he jogs away before forcing myself to get into the car. I've already mentioned that gossip in Joyville is a recognized sport, and watching his ass is definitely something that will get me noticed and talked about. Right now, all people can say is that we were talking outside the pizza place. If I start drooling in the street, the talk will get a lot more intense.

I turn on the engine and watch in the mirror, waiting for Dom to pass me, then pull out after him. He doesn't live far from the town center—not that anything in Joyville is really far —and soon we're turning into the underground parking garage of a condo building. He waves me toward a section clearly marked Visitor, and I park quickly, then go meet him at the elevator.

When we get upstairs to his place, I'm taken aback by how spacious it is. I mean, I didn't expect him to live in a poky box, but it really feels huge—if I hadn't seen the door for another unit on this floor, I would have assumed it took up the whole level. I guess the floor-to-ceiling windows add to the openness of it.

Dom shows me into the kitchen, where we deposit the food on the counter, and he gets out some plates and napkins. "Do you mind if I go change?" he asks.

"Not at all," I assure him. "As long as you don't mind if I take my shoes off."

"Go for it. In fact, I can lend you some sweats if you want to change?"

Take off my clothes in his apartment? The temptation would be too strong. "Thanks, but I'm good."

He begins walking backward toward the hallway. "Okay, well help yourself to a beer—they're in the fridge. I'll be back in a sec and we'll watch that episode of *Poldark*." He disappears, and I turn to the fridge and help myself to a beer, grabbing one for him too. There's no TV in here, so I'm guessing he's okay with us eating in the living room. I cart the food and plates in there, kick off my shoes, then hesitate. Maybe I should have waited in the kitchen instead of making myself so completely at home?

I'm still dithering over it when he comes in. "Oh, great—you've got us all set up. Thanks." He drops onto the couch, turns on the TV, then loads up a plate with one hand while browsing through menus with the remote in the other. "Sit, be comfortable."

He doesn't have to ask me twice. I settle at the other end of the couch, grab my plate, and dig in to the food.

"Okay, here it is," he says. "Start from the beginning?"

"Please don't tell me you're one of those people who can start a series halfway through," I say, widening my eyes in mock horror, and he smirks.

"Yep. I also like spoilers."

"People like you will bring about the apocalypse."

He laughs so hard, he snorts, and I love the utter imperfection of it.

"Start from the beginning," I order when he finally stops chuckling, and he points the remote at the TV.

"You're the boss."

I make myself keep quiet as the show begins, something that's really difficult for me. I'm one of those people who likes to keep up a running commentary when watching a movie or TV show with someone else. I want to hear what they think and share my thoughts. But most people hate that, and I'm not quite ready to scare Dom off yet, so I stuff my face and let him watch in peace.

The food's been decimated by the time the credits roll, and I glance over at him. "Ready for that trashy reality show yet?" I want to ask if he liked it, but honestly, I don't think I have to. He seemed really engrossed, not at all like he was bored and just waiting for it to finish.

"Sneaky bastard," he grumbles. "Okay, let's watch more."

I crow in victory, not at all a gracious winner. "Yes!" He starts the next episode, and this time we talk, him asking questions and me explaining where things differ from the novels. When we get to the end of the second episode, he willingly concedes that he's going to keep watching.

"But not tonight," he adds. "Let's grab the ice cream and watch something so mindless that we can… talk through it."

That tiny hesitation, paired with the look he gives me, tells me very clearly that not only are we not hanging out as buddies, but that we won't be talking, either.

"Ice cream," I agree, sounding just a little bit breathless, and his smile sends a shiver through me.

We gather the remnants of dinner from the coffee table and haul it to the kitchen. "Grab the ice cream from the freezer, will you, while I put the garbage in the laundry room." He's back a moment later, in time to see me pondering whether triple fudge swirl or raspberry and white chocolate would be the better choice.

"What are you doing?" He sounds amused.

"Trying to choose. Which do you prefer?"

He makes a scoffing sound. "Choose? We don't choose in this house. We take it all."

I'm still processing that when he sweeps both containers from my hands, opens them, and proceeds to scoop some of each into both bowls. "There. The perfect solution."

I stare at the bowls while he puts the ice cream away. "It does seem like it," I agree. "Although I'll admit that your house motto of 'we take it all' does concern me a little. What happens when you and Cara both want ice cream and there's only a tiny bit left?"

His grin lights his whole face as he turns back to me. "Pitched battles. She used to win because she'd play the little girl card and start to cry crocodile tears, but now that she's older, that doesn't work. Now it's my turn to win, because I'm the parent and I have the power to ground her."

I can't help the laugh that bubbles up. I grab my bowl and head back toward the living room, shaking my head. "That would definitely be interesting to watch. Ridiculous, but interesting."

He follows me, and as we settle back onto the couch, a little closer to each other this time, he says, "Taste the ice cream first, and then tell me it's ridiculous for me to fight my daughter for it."

Rolling my eyes at the challenge in his stare, I scoop up a little bit of each flavor and put the spoon in my mouth. Sweet, creamy deliciousness explodes over my tongue, and I moan.

Yes. I actually *moan* over ice cream.

Dom smirks. "See?" He digs into his, and for a moment, there's silence as we concentrate on scarfing down this incredible treat. I have to find out where he gets it from—the cartons didn't look like mass-produced store stuff.

"You've got a little…"

I look up to see him gesture to my face. Oh, crap… am I wearing my food in my beard? How embarrassing. I wipe my chin, but he shakes his head and scoots closer.

"Almost, but… let me." His thumb swipes slowly at the corner of my mouth, and my breath hitches. He presses his thumb against my lips. "Fudge," he whispers. "Don't waste it."

I'm not thinking when my tongue strokes along his flesh, tasting the tiny hint of chocolate fudge and the warm, salty-sweet flavor of Dom's skin.

I swallow hard. His eyes are intent on my face.

So I suck his thumb into my mouth. "Mmm."

A tiny smile quirks his lips. "Want something else to suck on?"

I grin, releasing his thumb, and by unplanned mutual agreement, we lean in for a kiss. His mouth tastes even better than his thumb—probably because of the ice cream, but I like to think part of it is just *him*.

One kiss turns into more, the minutes blurring together into a haze of touch and rising arousal—

"Crap!" I jerk away from him.

"What?" He blinks dazedly, sending a smug glow through me, but I resist the temptation to take his mouth again. It's easier than you'd think, seeing I've got a lapful of melting ice cream.

Cringing, I pick up both bowls—because yes, *both* somehow ended up in my lap—and use a spoon to try to scrape up the melted, sticky, cold mess.

"Oh, shit. I'm so sorry. I guess I wasn't paying attention. Hold on, let me…" He takes the bowls and hurries into the kitchen to deposit them in the sink. A moment later, he's back, handing me a dish towel. "Uh, this probably sounds self-serving, but I think you need to take your pants off."

I snort, tossing aside the towel. "Is this a movie starring Rock Hudson and Doris Day? Are you manipulating me into taking my clothes off so you can take advantage?" I stand and unfasten and unzip my pants. Dom laughs a little, but he seems to be having trouble keeping his eyes on my face.

He wants me. That's so sexy.

I don't bother with a striptease or trying to be seductive; I just drop my pants, then bend over to scoop them up. "Laundry room? Mind if I wipe these off?" I'm so glad I'm wearing a new pair of boxer briefs. They fit really well, and although my body isn't pin-up material, I've never had any complaints.

He swallows hard, blinks, then seems to realize I asked him a question. "Why don't I just throw them in the wash? You don't mind hanging around here for a few hours, do you?" The unspoken part of the question —*naked, with me*—hangs in the air.

Remember how I said I don't really miss sex when

I'm not having it? That's still true, but when there's the promise of sex, I really, really want it. Now. This second.

I drop my pants, pull my shirt off over my head and drop it too, then look Dom right in the eye and hook my thumbs into the waistband of my underwear. They hit the floor a second later.

"Fuck yeah," he says, stripping off his shirt as he closes the gap between us. Our mouths are fused together in the next second as he fumbles with his pants. I don't mind the delay; it gives me time to get my hands on him. He's toned all over, his midtone skin covered in just enough dark hair to be sexy. I like it. And from the sound he makes, he likes the way I'm rubbing up against him.

In the next moment, we're back on the couch, me stretched out on my back with him over me, between my legs.

And then he yanks himself away. "Wait. Before… supplies."

It's my turn to blink dazedly as he scrambles up and races toward the hallway. What…?

He's back a moment later with a bottle of lube and a handful of condoms. *Ohhh*. I can't help snickering, though.

"What?"

I nod to the hand holding the condoms. "That's a bit ambitious."

He looks down, then laughs. "I didn't bother to count, just grabbed." He dumps them on the coffee table with the lube, then crawls back onto the couch, propping himself over me on his elbows. "Now," he murmurs, "where were we?"

I hook a hand around his neck to pull his mouth to

mine, but he wriggles down and plants a kiss on my collarbone instead. My hand slides into his hair, and I leave it there as he kisses and licks his way down my chest. The strands are soft and cool against my fingers, unlike his hot, hot tongue on my nipples.

By the time he gets to my cock, I'm a writhing, whimpering mess. It's been a long time since someone spent time just touching me without racing toward the goal line.

And then he sucks me into his hot, wet mouth, and all I want is to race toward that goal. Everything is hazy except his mouth sucking my dick, his hand on my balls —*oh, fuck!*—and his iron-hard cock leaking against my calf.

So close... so—

He pulls off. "If you come now, will you be too sensitive for a fuck?"

It takes forever for the haze of arousal to clear enough for me to understand.

"No." I suck in a breath. "I like it." It's true. It all feels a little more intense that way. When I was younger, I used to be able to come again from being fucked after coming, no hands.

He grins, and there's something just a bit wicked about it. "Good."

I wonder if, now that I've had this tiny respite, I can hold off for a while longer, but then he swallows me deep, taking me right down his throat, and there's no way in hell I can hold back.

Every muscle in my body tenses so hard, it almost hurts, and I come. It's without doubt the best orgasm I've had in years, and when it's finally over, I can't move a muscle.

Holy… Dom has some amazing skills. Is this what they teach in business school? Maybe I should have been looking for dates in the corporate world years ago.

As my mind floats and my body attempts to recover, I hear a familiar *snick* sound.

"Oliver?" Dom murmurs near my ear.

"Mmmm?" Words are hard.

"Still up for a fuck?"

I want to laugh, but that would take energy. Instead, a huff escapes me. "Not gonna be up for a long time after that. But yeah. Fuck me." If he's as good at that as he is with his mouth, this should feel good—and prolong my sex stupor.

He kisses me, which is nice, but cold lube-wet fingers trace my hole, and I flinch.

"Sorry. I'll try to warm it a bit."

The next touch is much better, ghosting over sensitive skin. I shiver a little as one finger probes gently, then slides in, teasing, testing. It really does feel so much more intense right after an orgasm, but I love it. I force my eyes open so I can see Dom's face. He's concentrating intently, a tiny frown line between his brows, and it's the sexiest thing ever. I focus on staying relaxed and am rewarded by another finger stretching me.

"Mmm."

His gaze shifts to my face. "Good?" he asks, his voice a little hoarse. He wants this. Me.

"Yeah." I'm probably not quite loose enough yet, but I like the burn. "I'm ready."

"But—"

I squeeze around his fingers, and he gasps, sweat visibly breaking out on his forehead.

"Come on, Dom. I'm ready."

He doesn't look entirely convinced but withdraws his fingers and reaches for the condoms. Faster than I would have thought possible, he's back, gloved up and slick with lube as the thick head of his cock nudges against my hole.

I shiver again. "Go on." I keep my eyes on his face as he presses forward past the initial resistance. He's panting a little as he eases in, and I revel in the combination of his desire and the burn/stretch. "Dom," I whisper, and he groans, jerking forward the last little bit.

He drops his head to rest on my shoulder. "Fuck me," he croaks, and I chuckle. "Oh, fuck, fuck, I can feel…"

Nudging him, I say, "What are you waiting for?"

His whole body shudders, then he lifts his head and meets my gaze. "Are you good? Not too sensitive?"

Gathering energy I didn't know I still had, I lean up, pause at the incredible sensation the shift causes, and kiss him. "Fuck me. Hard. Now." I drop back prone and smile at him. "Do it."

And he does.

I was right. It feels amazing. He's a god. I lie there, admiring the view and floating on endorphins as he strokes all my nerve endings in the *best* way. He nails my prostate a few times, and it's almost too much, just a shade past stimulating, but… is it wrong that I still like it?

Then he thrusts a final time and comes, his back bowing with the force of it, and it's so damn hot.

I DRIFT AWAKE SLOWLY, stretching a little. I'm not entirely comfortable—I think I've fallen asleep on the couch, and whoever I'm sharing it wi— Whoa!

Suddenly, I'm wide awake, and then a second later, it all floods back to me. Oh. I'm at Dom's. We had sex.

"What?" he murmurs beside me, obviously having felt me tense up—or maybe I accidentally elbowed him as I woke up.

"Nothing." I extract myself from around him and sit up. "We fell asleep, I guess." I cringe because I'm a little sticky and crusty with cum. We must have crashed out hard for me to not clean up first.

"Mmm." Dom stirs, then sits up too, his chest pressing against my back and his arms snaking around me. "Just a little powernap." He kisses the side of my neck, the roughness of his stubble making me shiver. "Want a shower?"

"Uh…" Is this his way of asking me to get cleaned up and leave? "That would be great." Either way, I'm not turning down the chance to wash up. If he wants me to go after, fine. If not… also fine.

"Come on, then." He slides out from behind me, snagging my hand and pulling me up. "I can't wait to get my hands all over your soaped up, wet body."

Oh, now that sounds like a great idea. I follow him through the apartment, shooting a glance down at my cock. There's no way I'm getting it up again tonight, but that doesn't mean I can't feel really, really good—and make him feel good too.

But before that…

"Dom," I begin as he lets go of my hand to start the shower in what is frankly the most amazing bathroom I've ever seen.

"Yeah? How hot do you want the water?"

"Just short of scalding," I reply, distracted by the thoughtful question, "but it's fine if you like it cooler."

He flashes me a grin. "Hot works for me too." As he turns to open a cupboard and pull out some fluffy towels, I push aside the swoony sigh and remind myself of my purpose.

"Dom, I want to make sure we're on the same page here."

He stops and gives me his full attention. "What page is that?"

I hesitate. "I like you. You're charming, funny, intelligent, and basically more attractive than any man has the right to be. In different circumstances, I'd be all over you —especially after that orgasm. But your daughter is a student at my school, and you're the director, and…" I peter out, not sure how to explain it.

Fortunately, he nods. "Yeah. I get it. Honestly, I didn't realize how big an impact I'd have on this town. The company, sure, but before I got here, it never occurred to me how much the town depended on the company and that I would be the focus of so much attention. I wouldn't want to drag anyone else into that spotlight unless they wanted it too." He leans over and kisses me, a warm kiss that's not a precursor to anything. "I like you. I don't have many friends here, and I work with all the others. It's nice to talk to a smart man with a good sense of humor without having to worry about maintaining just a tiny bit of distance in case I have to draw a line about something in the office. And it's really nice to have sex with someone I like and not have to worry that they want to move in and that the gossip tree or whatever is going to start laying bets on when we get married." He stops and swallows, and I realize that this is really important to him—just as much as it is to me. "So I guess the page I'm on is that I want to be friends, and I want to fuck sometimes, but I don't want to cause any complications that are going to rock this town."

A weight lifts off my chest. Don't misunderstand— there's a tiny bit of regret there too, because I would like someone to cuddle up with every night and make plans for the holidays with. And yeah, part of me wants it to be Dom… but none of me wants it to be the director.

"That sounds perfect," I murmur. "Friends who fuck. Let's do that."

He laughs, and I don't think I'm fooling myself when I say his relief is mixed with sadness, but then we're kissing again as the bathroom fills with steam, and I let everything else float away.

SEVEN

Dom

_____

Never again am I letting myself go so long without sex.

Yeah, yeah, my hand does an adequate job of releasing the pressure, but it's not the same as hot, sweaty flesh-on-flesh contact with another person. And it had definitely been way too long, because I went off like a teenager last night. I can't remember being that horny in ages.

Of course, my choice of partner might have had something to do with that. Oliver really is fucking hot. I never thought I had a professor kink, but I guess I do. He's also a lot of fun to talk to, and I can foresee many great evenings where we relax and blow off steam together—as well as blowing other things. Friends with benefits is always so much nicer than just a random hookup.

Am I just a tiny bit disappointed that it's just going to be friends with benefits? Kind of. I mean, this is the first Saturday in a long time that I haven't had to work. Cara won't be home from her friend's house until much later. It would have been nice to spend the morning snuggling in bed and then have a leisurely breakfast and make plans for the day, but that's couple-y kind of stuff. I guess Cara really was right to worry that I'll be lonely when she's gone, because I'm already feeling a little lonely just knowing what I'm missing out on.

We made the right decision not to date, though. He doesn't need to be dragged into the "director" spotlight. Since Cara and I had that conversation, I've become hyperaware of how I'm treated around town, and there definitely is something there. It's a weird combination of awe, respect, and fear, and honestly, it's hard to take. People who don't know me, who I'll likely never meet, are dependent on me—in a roundabout way. I've headed companies before, but never in this unique kind of situation where a whole town basically hangs in the balance. And things aren't helped by the fact that the director before me was let go for incompetence and the company has been in a state of upheaval over the past six months. Everyone's afraid that things might go bad, despite assurances that it's all under control.

So, yeah… for now, at least, it's probably better that I'm seen to be focused only on work.

Midafternoon on Tuesday, there's a knock on my office doorframe, and I look up to see Derek.

"Hey, come in." I have an open door policy—literally—but even if I didn't, Derek doesn't usually disturb me unless it's important. His district is in the best shape of all of them, so aside from our planning and strategy sessions, I haven't had to work with him as closely as with some of the others.

He strolls in, a smirk on his face that makes me just a little suspicious, and settles into my visitor chair, leaning back and crossing his legs.

"What's up?" I ask, suddenly wary. I have a strong urge to check my fly—knowing my luck, it's been undone all day or something.

"Oh, nothing much. I just thought you might like to hear some interesting gossip that's making the rounds."

I raise a brow. "There's interesting gossip going around and Layla hasn't told me yet?" I raise my voice. "Layla?"

A second later, she appears in the doorway. "Did you tell him yet?" she asks Derek.

Whoa.

"Not yet," he says, just as I ask,

"You know about this and you haven't told me?" I'm in genuine shock—I thought Layla told me all the gossip.

She winces. "I wasn't sure how you'd take it."

Dread forms a hard knot in my stomach. "Is it bad?"

Derek laughs. "No. Layla, relax. He's going to be fine with it—and this way, we might get some confirmation."

Oh… a lightbulb clicks on in my brain.

"It's about me, huh? Okay, hit me with it."

Layla comes to perch on the other visitor chair. "It's going around town that on Friday night, you had a date with one of the teachers from the high school."

I shake my head. "It wasn't a date. I ran into him when I went to order a pizza, and we ended up hanging out and eating together. That's all."

"Oh." Layla sounds disappointed, but Derek's still smirking.

"Is this the same teacher Luke was talking about? The English teacher you spoke to about Cara?" He shoots a sideways glance at Layla, and I'm grateful that he's chosen his words so carefully. I trust Layla to maintain confidences, but I'm not interested in discussing my love life—wannabe or otherwise—with her.

"Yes. You remember, Layla, that I wasn't pleased with Mrs. Hamilton? Oliver helped me resolve the issue and get Cara moved to another class."

She nods. "I guess it's a shame when two people can't have a casual dinner as friends without the whole town turning it into something else," she says, then sighs. "Are you sure you wouldn't like to date him? He's such a nice man—my youngest has him now, and my oldest had him for two classes back when she was at the school. I think the two of you could be good for each other, and god knows, you need something other than work and your daughter in your life."

"You sound just like Cara," I tell her, then groan. "Oh, fuck. This is probably all over the school. Cara's going to kill me."

Derek winces, but Layla just hums. "I think you'll be okay. Nothing I've heard mentioned that you have a kid at the school—most people don't know that. I reckon they just think the two of you met somewhere in town."

"I hope so. You're right, Layla—he's a nice man, and he'll make a good friend." There. Hopefully that lays some groundwork for us to hang out occasionally. If we're friends—and nobody can object to us being friends—then there's a good reason for us to be coming and going from each other's places.

A look of sheer determination crosses Layla's face. "I'll start telling people not to make mountains out of molehills, but just so you know, my vote is for you to take that nice man on a date. If you ever decide to do that, let me know and I'll make the reservations and everything. I'll make sure it's a magical evening."

Derek clears his throat, and a glance at his face shows that he's trying not to laugh.

"Thanks, Layla. I'll keep that in mind, but we really are just friends."

She heaves another disappointed sigh, then gets up and goes back out to her desk. Derek waits a moment, then leans forward and says, "I had to beat Luke and Grant in three rounds of rock-paper-scissors to be the one to come in here, so I'm gonna need a little more than 'we're just friends.' Especially since they're both waiting in my office for the update."

He's joking. "You're joking." Right?

He shakes his head. "It gets worse. After we had dinner that night, I told Trav"—his boyfriend—"about our conversation. He immediately thought of six different people he could set you up with. I talked him out of it, but he still talked about it with Dimi and Jason."

This is getting out of control. "Why?" I ask, incredulity dripping from my tone. I know who Dimi and Jason are—Dimi heads up the Joy Village Theater Company and has the same seniority as the other department heads. Jason is the ex-Broadway director who was headhunted to direct JVTC's shows.

He shrugs. "They work together every day. It came up. The important thing is, Dimi is arguably the biggest gossip in the state—he gives Layla a run for her money.

He was born in this town, he knows pretty much everyone who lives here, and his mother has a finger in every pie in Joyville."

My stomach sinks. "I think I've met her," I mutter, remembering the charming woman who brought me a welcome basket right after I moved here and informed me that everyone would love to see me get involved with the town. "Sascha Weston?" I never made the connection between the names before now. Weston isn't exactly an uncommon name.

"That's her," Derek confirms. "Dimi always denies it, but he is just like his mother. So now he's texting me every fifteen minutes—" As if on cue, his phone chimes. "—to ask why I haven't told him what's going on. If I don't have something for him soon, he's going to come down here and ask for a meeting with you on some made-up pretext, and then before you know it, you'll be telling him things you never thought you'd ever tell anyone."

I chuckle-snort, but Derek just gives me an I-warned-you look and sits back in his chair. Groaning, I scrub my hands over my face.

"Can Dimi be trusted to keep a secret?" I ask, even as the sensible part of me demands to know what I'm doing.

He nods. "We tell him the public line is just friends, and he'll stick to that. Fair warning, he'll want to start a betting pool—but someone's probably already done that. Toby's been looking particularly smug today."

Nobody from my old life would believe this.

I groan again, then say, "Oliver and I are friends. We really did run into each other at the pizza place and decide to hang out. Cara was at a sleepover, and it made sense to watch TV and eat pizza together."

He rolls his wrist expectantly. "And?"

I hesitate, and he flashes his most charming smile. Admittedly, it's pretty good. I instantly feel a sense of liking and camaraderie for him. That thing should be weaponized.

"Come on, Dom. I was there that night when you said you were interested in him."

I'm not sure if that's exactly what I said, but I remember we definitely discussed it. "And we agreed that neither of us wants to date, but we'll be friends and help each other out." I can't bring myself to use the term fuck buddy in the office. I just can't. I'm supposed to be the arbiter of professional behavior here.

Derek nods, still smiling. "That's great. I'm glad you're making connections and friendships here. And we'll do what we can to keep the gossip minimal for you both."

"I'd prefer none—doesn't anyone have anything better to talk about?" I grumble, and he laughs.

"Yeah, don't we all wish. Listen, you and Cara should come to our place for brunch Saturday."

The abrupt change of subject makes me blink. "Brunch?"

He nods. "Yeah. With Trav and Dimi and Jason working most nights, dinner is usually out, but we've been trying to all get together for brunch every so often. Luke and Grant bring the kids, so Cara won't be the only teenager there. You should come."

"Uh, thanks. I'll ask Cara, but that sounds good."

He flashes that killer smile again. "Great. And that'll get Dimi off my back."

Before I can come up with a response, he's up and on his way to the door. "Thanks, Dom. I'll text you the details."

I've been had. Oh, well—it's not the end of the world. After all, Dimi can ask as many questions as he likes, but I don't have to answer. And if Luke's kids and Cara are there, he's going to be limited in what he does, right? So I can enjoy breakfast and the company and not worry about the rest.

In the meantime, I should check in with Oliver and make sure he's not being harassed about this. Not that there's a lot I can do if he is… but it's the right thing to do. And he should probably know what my "official" line is.

It's got nothing to do with the fact that I've been wanting to text him for four days. I wonder if he'd be up for sexting and some dirty pics? Our time together is going to be limited, and I wouldn't mind adding to my spank bank for whenever we can't be together.

Dom: Hi—hope you're having a good day. Just found out that people have been talking about us dating. My assistant is the gossip queen, and I've told her we're just friends. Is that okay with you?

I know he probably won't see it right away if he's in class, but at least I've covered that base.

It's only half an hour before he replies.

Oliver: Hi! Thanks for texting. My friend Jaiden was very excited to fill me in on the rumors. He knows the truth because it's impossible to keep secrets from him, but he's promised to tell everyone we ran into each other by accident and are just friends. So we're on the same page—again.

I read it twice, smiling. I like the idea of him having a friend he tells everything to.

Dom: Some of my friends know the truth too. Don't worry, I trust them all.

Wow, that felt weird to type, but it really is true. I see the three dots begin their dance, and don't bother to put my phone down.

Oliver: No problem. Did Cara tell you she and her friends made their presentation on changing the extra-credit system?

Dom: No. I knew it was happening soon, but not exactly when. Were you impressed?

Oliver: Blown away. And honestly, I felt so guilty that I hadn't already done something about it.

Dom: From what I've heard, you're a good teacher who doesn't let bias affect you. Had you even realized the extent of the problem?

Oliver: Not really. And that makes it worse, because I should have.

Dom: Cut yourself some slack. You trusted the teachers in your department to grade fairly. You can't micromanage them. Now you know it's an issue, and you'll fix it.

Oliver: I suppose. I'm just glad I only have to deal with my department. Can't imagine having to manage a whole company, like you do.

Dom: I didn't start out with a company this big. My first management job was a team of six. It hurts less when you ease into it ;-)

I stare at the screen. Did I just send a winky face and a sex pun in a conversation about team management? It's been way too long since I did this flirting thing.

Oliver: LOL

The dots jump around a bit more, but he's either composing an essay or writing and deleting texts, so I seize the initiative.

Dom: Doing anything tonight? How do you feel about phone sex?

The dots disappear. Have I scared him off? I hope not.

Oliver: Nine o'clock work for you?

Yeah, baby.

CARA'S WAITING for me when I get home. And I don't mean in the kitchen doing homework, or with dinner half-prepared. No, she's standing right inside the front door, arms crossed, face determined.

I know that look. It never bodes well for me.

"Hey," I say, closing the door behind me. "What's wrong?" I'm playing dumb just in case she's mad at someone else. No point digging my own grave.

"What's *wrong?*" she echoes. "Seriously, Dad? Did you honestly just ask me what's wrong when I had to find out at school that you had dinner with Mr. Jeffries on Friday?"

I wince and start toward my room. She follows me with a level of doggedness that only a pissed-off teenager can manage.

"Nobody's made the connection between you and me, have they?" I ask, concerned. I really don't want her school life to be difficult—more difficult—because of me. I set my laptop bag on the chair in the corner of my bedroom and kick off my shoes.

"No, but that's not the point. How could you not tell me you had a date, Dad? Honestly, I can't believe you're keeping secrets like I'm a little kid. How did it go?"

I freeze while digging through a drawer for a T-shirt. Did she just…? I turn around and meet her gaze.

There's still a lot of annoyance there, but also… excitement? Anticipation?

This is so weird.

"Wait… you're not mad because people are saying Oliver and I are dating?"

There it is… the expression that says I'm so stupid, and she can't believe she has a parent who's so dense. I haven't seen that in a while—who knew I'd missed it?

"Why would I be upset about that? I *told* you to start dating, remember? But the least you could do is have the courtesy to tell me you're seeing someone."

Oh my god. I literally do not know what to say.

"I'm… not."

She scrunches up her face. "You're not what?"

"Not seeing someone. Oliver and I bumped into each other at the pizza place and decided to eat together. That's all. We're just friends."

Do I feel bad for lying to my daughter? Yes. It actually makes my chest feel tight. But I'm not prepared to tell her that I have a friends-with-benefits arrangement with a teacher from her school who she's likely to run into occasionally.

"Ohhhh." Her disappointment makes me feel like crap. "Really? That's too bad. I really like him, and I bet you two would be great together."

Jesus fucking Christ, it's like I'm paying for all my sins at once. Could I possibly feel any worse than I do right now?

"Sorry, honey," I manage through a tight throat. "He's a really nice guy, and we get along well, but…" I shrug.

She chews on her lip thoughtfully. "Maybe something will develop? If you both hang out, I mean. Do you find him at all attractive? That geeky academic vibe he's got going is kind of hot."

Yes. Yes, I could feel worse. We could add shock and horror to the plethora of emotions roiling through me.

"Cara, do you want me to date him, or are you trying to tell me that you want to?"

She laughs, and I have no words to tell you what a relief that is.

"Don't be stupid, Dad. Just because I can objectively recognize that he's attractive doesn't mean I'm attracted. I'm not into much older guys."

"You have no idea how glad I am to hear that," I say dryly. "Have you started dinner?"

Rolling her eyes, she says, "I'll go do it now. But this conversation is not over!"

As she stomps away toward the kitchen, I close my bedroom door and use the time while I'm changing out of my work clothes to try and come up with ways to distract her. I still haven't got anything that might work when I enter the kitchen a few minutes later.

Cara's stabbing potatoes with a fork, which likely means we're having microwave baked potatoes and salad for dinner. It's a favorite for when neither of us can be bothered to spend a lot of time on cooking. I grab the lettuce and some veggies out of the fridge and start preparing the salad.

"How was school today? Did you do anything other than listen to rumors?" I've decided that the best defense is offense—I just have to keep her talking about something else so she won't think about my dating life.

"The rumors took over most of the day," she admits. "It's so weird to have everyone talking about my dad like that, even if they don't know you're my dad. But we also had that appointment with Mr. Jeffries to present our proposal for the new extra-credit system."

"I—" Fuck, that was close. If I tell her I know, she's going to know I've been talking to Oliver today. I clear my throat, hoping that will cover my blunder. "How did it go?" I ask instead.

Her grin lights up her face. "Good. He agrees that it needs to change and said he'd get the process started. I'm not sure exactly who has to approve it—the principal or the school board, maybe?—but there's probably a procedure or something."

"Probably," I agree. "That's great news, Cara. I'm so proud of the way you've dealt with this particular issue." My tone is almost as pointed as the words I use, and she rolls her eyes.

"Yeah, Dad, I get it. I've been trying harder to be reasonable and pick my battles." She puts the potatoes in the microwave and starts readying the toppings. I take a big step sideways and bump her shoulder with mine.

"I know you have. I think this is a great example of how taking a different approach got you what you wanted in the end. You're going to go far in life, Cara, whatever you choose to do."

This time, her smile is smaller, a little shy, but just as rewarding for me. "Thanks, Dad. But don't think I've forgotten what we were talking about before."

I groan and seriously think about throwing some shredded carrot at her. "Cara, you're just going to have to let that go. Isn't it enough that I've been making friends? By the way, we've been invited to brunch this Saturday."

"Brunch?" She sounds a combination of intrigued and baffled. "Why brunch? And who with?"

"One of my colleagues invited me—one of the ones I had dinner with when you stayed over at the school the other week. And it's brunch because his boyfriend and some of the other people coming work in the theater and nights aren't good for them."

"They work in the theater? That sounds kind of cool. Is it going to be all old people, though?"

Anyone who says kids keep you young has no fucking clue what they're talking about. The only time I ever feel like an old man is when I'm talking to my daughter. I'm forty-eight, for fuck's sake, not a hundred and eight.

"Old?"

She shrugs. "You know what I mean."

"Choose your words more carefully, child, or you'll discover the power we *old* people have. And no, Luke's bringing his kids—you said you know one of them. Mila?"

"Oh, that's okay. I can talk to her if the conversation about dentures and hip replacements gets boring." She snickers, and I shake my head.

"I'll tell Derek we're coming, then. And I'll have you know I spend a fortune at the dentist so I won't have to wear dentures." Damn it, I didn't mean to say that.

She nods solemnly. "Actually, one of the things people said today was that you have a nice smile. They were passing around a picture someone took of you and Mr. Jeffries at the pizza place."

Whoa.

"There are *pictures*? Someone took a picture of us waiting for pizza?" That's so creepy. I mean… I'm not famous. Neither is Oliver. I'm a businessman, and he's an English teacher. That doesn't warrant paparazzi-type stalking.

"Yeah, it was really weird. But you guys looked like you were enjoying yourselves, and when you smile, you don't look like a robot, so…" She shrugs again. "I was kind of worried that someone would recognize you from the reading, but I guess nobody put it together."

"It must be the suit," I say dryly. "My super-effective disguise." I can't believe people took pictures and are sharing them. I really want to call Oliver and see if he knows.

The microwave dings, and I push it all to the back of my mind for now.

I CLOSE MY BEDROOM DOOR, lock it, and then make myself comfortable on my bed. Cara's in her room, and it's not likely she'll disturb me, but I'm not taking any risks—which means I'm making this call, because I don't want her to hear the phone ring and come ask me who it is.

Yes, I'm being paranoid. The chances of that happening are slim to none. But I didn't get to where I am in life by not preparing for every eventuality.

I bring up the FaceTime app and call Oliver. He answers on the first ring, which is gratifying.

"Hi." He sounds a little bit breathless, and I smile.

"Hey. Is this a good time?"

"Yes." He clears his throat. "So…"

Suddenly, I feel shy. This is far from the first time I've had phone sex, but it seems different—maybe because we basically made an appointment. Maybe we just need to ease into it so it feels more natural.

"Uh, hey, so I just found out that someone took a picture of us at the pizza place on Friday and now it's being passed around. Did you know about it?"

He blinks, those lovely brown eyes widening. "No. Although, now that I know, that clears up a lot of the things that were said today. I was starting to think the whole school had been in the restaurant with us and I somehow didn't see any of them."

"Derek and Layla didn't say anything about it to me. I found out from Cara. Maybe it was a student who took it and it's mostly just at the school?"

"Possibly." He shrugs. "It's a little daunting to know someone did that, but it doesn't change anything. Right?"

I nod. "Right. I just really hate that someone violated your privacy like that. If this starts to cause trouble for you at work, let me know."

"And what are you going to do?" he teases, flashing a smile.

I open my mouth to reply, then close it again. "I have no idea," I admit. "What a shame I can't ground other people's kids."

He snorts. "I hear you. Speaking of kids, there's no chance Cara could walk in, is there? Because I'd really, really like to avoid that. Ever."

"Door's locked," I assure him. "She's in her room, and she hardly ever comes out at this time on a weeknight. We're completely and totally private. Just you and me." I quirk an eyebrow at him. "Wanna take off your shirt?"

He grins, a flash of white teeth, then takes off his

shirt. It's not like last time, which was a race to get naked. This time he takes his time, teasing me. It works too—I'm completely naked before he's done, hard and ready to go.

His chuckle goes straight to my dick, the husky sound turning me on way more than it probably should. "Okay, I can take a hint." He strips off the rest of his clothes while I grab the lube and prop my phone against a couple of pillows, allowing me to be hands free—because I plan to need them.

When we're both settled, naked, on our respective beds, I let my gaze skate over him. Even in miniature form on the phone screen, he cranks my engine.

"My, my," I say, "looks like you're glad to see me."

He wraps his hand around his dick and squeezes. "Oh yeah. My friend here remembers exactly how much fun you are."

"Yeah?" I stroke my fingers lightly over my own cock, not ready to take a firm grip yet. A shiver overtakes me as I feather the same touch over my balls.

Oliver groans, sliding his hand lazily up and down. "You're so hot when you're turned on."

"So are you. Just looking at that fat, hard prick is enough to make my ass feel empty."

His breathing speeds up. So does his hand. My dick throbs, and I close my hand around it. "You like to be fucked?"

"Oh, yeah." I adjust my position so he has a good view of me jerking with one hand and teasing my hole with the other. "Don't... get me wrong—" I pause to breathe. "—I love driving into a hot, tight ass, but... sometimes I want... to be the one getting... my prostate pegged." I give myself a squeeze and let my head drop back, then jerk it up again. I don't want to miss a second of watching Oliver. He's moving faster now, panting, eyes glued to the show I'm giving him, clearly loving it—

I come. It's faster than I expected, but I guess the triple stimulation—dick, ass, and visual—was too much for a long jerk session. Somewhere in the middle of it, I hear a stifled shout from Oliver, then a drawn-out groan, and knowing he's coming too makes it all so much more intense.

By the time my brain comes back online, I'm a quivering, breathless mess—literally. I must have given Oliver quite the cum shot.

I glance at my phone and see him sprawled back against his pillows, panting and smiling.

"We should call each other to say good night every day," he says.

I laugh. That's got my vote.

EIGHT

Oliver

_____

S ex is really good for stress.

The rumors about me and Dom die down pretty quickly, what with both of us saying we're just friends and also not really being seen together. Cara has an active social life, so we manage to hook up at least once most weeks, often twice, and then there's the phone sex. How did we cope before video chat? I can honestly say it's changed my life. It's so much nicer to get myself off when Dom's watching and talking dirty to me than it is alone.

So as Christmas begins its approach, Dom and I have been helping each other out for about a month, and I'm feeling the most relaxed that I have in years. I'm not ordinarily a tense person, but nothing fazes me now.

Jaiden's noticed, of course, and is constantly making snarky comments. He's happy for me, but I think also disappointed because we're not taking things any further. If it was up to him, Dom and I would be in the midst of a whirlwind romance, on the verge of announcing our engagement, and he'd be in charge of planning our wedding for next summer. When I dryly pointed out that I'm capable of planning my own wedding, thank you very much, and even if I wasn't, Dom or even Cara would be, he glared at me and announced that it was *his* fantasy and I should respect that.

Seriously. His fantasy… of my wedding. I think maybe he needs to spend some time and effort on spicing up his own relationship instead of dreaming one up for me.

Anyway, the bonus to great sex reducing stress levels is that Christmas shopping this year does not bother me at all. Usually it's at least a little bit daunting, but on this fine Saturday morning, I'm happily browsing through the shops on Main Street, hunting out the perfect gifts for my great-nieces and -nephews. I have four, all under the age of five, so they're actually pretty easy to impress. It's finding something that won't make their parents despair that's the challenge.

"Oliver?"

I turn and come face-to-face with Sascha Weston. I had two of her kids as my students, although the youngest is in his senior year of college now. Still, it's impossible to live in Joyville for a substantial amount of time and not at least know who Sascha Weston is. The woman is on practically every committee and still maintains an interest in the high school, even though nobody in her family attends right now.

"Sascha, good morning. How are you?"

She returns my smile and pats me on the arm. "Good, thanks. Doing some shopping?"

I shrug. "Yes. Christmas gifts, mostly. You?"

"Oh, no." She shakes her head. "I saw you from the street and came in to talk to you."

Alarm bells begin to go off in my head. Sascha has a gift for talking people—me—into things. You think you're going to say no, you can't possibly spend a day supervising the annual cat race or whatever, but then suddenly you've said yes and find yourself standing in the rain on a Sunday afternoon, watching cats do… something or other when you could have been curled up with a book.

True story.

"Well, it's always lovely to chat with you, but I really have to—"

She laughs. "Relax, Oliver. I really did just come to say hello. It's been a long time since we've talked."

I'm afraid to let down my guard, but I don't want to be rude—I genuinely like Sascha. "That's because you're always busy. Your own business, your family, all the committees… how do you find time to sleep, Sascha?"

"Pfft." She waves a hand. "Sleep is overrated. And the family is all grown up—grandma duties are a lot easier than mom ones."

We chat for a while longer about nothing in particular, and I'm finally beginning to relax when she goes in for the kill.

"You should come with me to my son's house this afternoon. He's having some people around, and they're wrapping the gifts for the holiday party. It was so kind of them to volunteer—you know how much the kids love opening those gifts."

And bam, she's got me. Seriously, how am I supposed to refuse? The town's annual holiday party on

Christmas Day was started to give people who couldn't get home for the holidays somewhere to go, and over the years—decades—it's turned into the only celebration the residents of Joyville want to have.

"Ahh…" I stall, desperately trying to think of an excuse. "I have plans tonight." And I do—Cara will be out, so Dom is coming over.

Sascha smiles. "Oh, that's fine, we should be done well before tonight. After all, many hands make light work!"

And that's how I end up in her car a few hours later. That's right, in her car, because the woman clearly doesn't trust me to follow through—she insisted on picking me up. And now she's chatting away about how glad she is she can rely on the community to step up and help with things like this. I barely get a word in, but I'm okay with that, because I don't really want to say that I don't want to contribute to the community. And honestly, I am glad to help out—it's just the way Sascha blindsides me that makes me uncomfortable. I do a lot of extracurricular volunteering at the school already, so it would be nice to actually be given the option to do more rather than being dragged into it.

Or so I tell myself as I follow her up to the front door of a nice townhouse. She doesn't knock, just opens the door and strolls in, calling out a hello as she leads me into the open-plan living-dining-kitchen space, where about a dozen people are scattered around, wrapping gifts.

It's a shock to realize I know some of them.

"How are we doing?" Sascha asks brightly. "I've brought you another volunteer. Oliver, you've met my son Dimi, haven't you?"

I look at the dark-haired, fair-skinned man coming toward me with an expression of avid excitement on his face that I don't understand. "I think so," I say uncertainly, extending my hand to shake. I'm pretty sure we have met before at a town function, but if I'm judging his age correctly, he would have been in college when I started teaching at Joyville High.

"It's great to see you," he declares enthusiastically. "So glad you could come. Thanks, Mom, Oliver is just what we needed."

There's a round of snickers from others in the room, and one outright laugh. Another man comes forward, shaking his head slightly and smiling indulgently at Dimi. He's around my age, and suddenly the pieces click together in my brain. I'd forgotten that Dimi Weston is in charge of the Joy Village Theater Company, and that he's living with the ex-Broadway director, Jason Phillips, who was headhunted from New York to work for the company.

"Dimi, ease up a little," he says. "Thanks for coming, Oliver. Any help we can get is appreciated. I'm Jason." He smiles at me, then transfers it to Sascha, and I don't think I'm imagining that it becomes a little stilted. "Are you staying, Sascha? Can I get you a drink?"

She waves a hand, and I'm definitely not imagining that she's not as vivacious as usual when she says, "No, I can't stay. I just came to bring Oliver and check in on how you're doing."

Wait…

"You're not staying?" I ask. "But you drove me here. If I'd known, I would have brought my car." Which I wanted to do, but she insisted on driving, claiming there would be parking issues what with all the volunteers.

She and Dimi exchange looks that have a frisson of concern racing down my spine, and then she says, "Not to worry, I'm sure someone here can drive you home." She backs away. "Okay, I'm off!" And in the next second, she's out of sight and I hear the thud of the front door closing.

I shake my head and look at Jason. "What just happened?"

"I'm so sorry" is all he says before Dimi seizes my arm and drags me farther into the room.

"Not to worry!" he declares, sounding just like his mom. "We'll definitely make sure you get home safely. Now, why don't we set you up right here?" I'm led over to the dining table. "I think you even know some of these people! Luke was just saying that Mila is in one of your classes." He pushes me into a chair as Luke makes a sympathetic face, but I can see that he's also trying not to laugh.

Dimi gives me a five-second rundown on what to do —wrap the pile of small gifts in the middle of the table —and then hightails it off to the kitchen counter, where Jason is standing with another pile and several rolls of wrapping paper.

I glance around the table at the amused faces surrounding me. "Hi." Luke and Grant, I know from that night at the school and also the parent-teacher conferences we had a few weeks ago. There are two more men, one of whom I recognize as Derek Bryer, who's been an assistant director at JU for years and who last year was involved in a very public murder debacle.

And sitting next to me is Dom.

He leans closer and murmurs, "I am *so* sorry. Dimi and his mom are clearly off their rockers."

I'm just wondering what he means by that—although I'm inclined to agree—when Derek smiles broadly and says, "It's nice to meet you. I'm Derek, and this is Trav." He gestures to the man beside him. "We've heard a lot about you."

I manage to smile back, although I'm definitely thrown off stride. "You have? That's... surprising."

Trav rolls his eyes, then winks. "They tell me you've lived here long enough to know that gossip is the town hobby," he says.

"Yeah, but I'm not—" My eyes go wide, and I look over at the kitchen counter. Dimi immediately turns away, as though he's been watching but doesn't want to get caught. Jason's shaking his head again. I turn to Dom. "Are they *matchmaking*?" I hiss, and he winces.

"Badly," Derek says, "but yeah, that would be my guess."

Oh my god. I thought the gossip about me and Dom dating had died. I thought it was over. Not that one of his employees and the town's queen of meddling would decide to matchmake!

Do they *know*? We thought we'd been so discreet, but maybe—

"Relax," Dom mutters. "All the adults in this room know we've been... friendly, but nobody's said anything to anyone else."

That's right, he has to qualify that the "adults" know, because there are five kids clustered around the coffee table in the living room doing their part for the community, including Cara, Mila, her boyfriend, and two preteen boys.

"Sascha?" I ask. If Sascha knows...

Dom looks across the table at Derek. "I don't know. I

don't think so? But then, I wasn't expecting her to bring you."

Trav half raises a hand. "I know." He keeps his voice low, probably because of the kids. "Sascha turned up at rehearsal the other day and grilled Dimi and us about Dom. She'd been thinking about all the rumors and had decided that if you"—he nods at Dom—"were really a nice person, then she wanted to push the two of you together, because you"—this time, he nods at me—"deserve love in your life and she wants to see you happy."

My jaw drops.

"Dimi, of course, thought that was an amazing idea, since he's been pouting about the fact that you both want to keep this casual and quiet. As far as I know, Sascha thinks you guys are just friends. Dimi is getting kind of scary about this whole thing, though, and I'm not sure it's safe to be around him anymore."

Dom groans.

"Hey, Mr. Jeffries!" Jamie, who I taught last year but isn't in any of my classes this year, leans between me and Dom to grab a roll of tape from the stack. "I didn't know you were coming today."

"Neither did I," I say dryly, then twist around to smile at him. "It's nice that you're helping out, Jamie."

He shrugs. "Yeah, well, I always liked getting my present from Santa when I was little. Only fair to pay it forward." He heads back to the group in the living room, and Luke sighs.

"I hate when he's all mature and thoughtful and reasonable," he mutters, and I choke back a laugh, momentarily distracted from my own drama.

Grant smirks. "I know, babe," he says mock-sympathetically. "How are you supposed to tell Mila he's no good and she should dump him when he's such a good kid?"

Luke smacks him in the pec. "Don't make it sound like I'm petty and stupid when I'm struggling to be a better person. Anyway, we're not here to talk about my problems. We're here to talk about Dom and Oliver's."

"We're not here to talk about anyone's problems," Dom says, grabbing for another of the little toys and starting to wrap it. "There are no problems here. Except maybe for Dimi."

"Don't worry about Dimi," Derek says. "We'll rein him in."

I muster up a grateful smile and begin wrapping presents. "Thanks, that would be appreciated. It's not that I'm not touched by Sascha's efforts"—although I'm more annoyed—"but it's really… unexpected."

The laugh that goes around the table gets Dimi's attention, and he watches us like a hawk for a moment. I can practically see him wondering what's so funny and if he should come over. Jason says something to him, and he reluctantly turns away.

The afternoon flies by. I won't ever admit it to Sascha, but I enjoy talking to these men, and it does feel good to be doing something for the community. I've seen how excited the kids get over these little token gifts from "Santa."

It's also really nice to be sitting next to Dom, feeling the low-level burn of anticipation for our night but not being able to touch or do anything. He's good company, and we have talked a lot over the past weeks, but it's always been one-on-one. We've never been in a group environment like this. It kind of makes me feel… naughty. I mean, some of them know that Dom and I are getting it on, but there are also people here who think we're just friends. So there's this underlying tension, the need to not let the secret out.

Maybe I just need to get out more. The person I spend the most time with in a social context is Jaiden, and that's dropped off lately with both of us being busy as the semester comes to an end—plus, I think he's having relationship problems. He hasn't wanted to talk about it, but there have been signs.

Anyway, by the time the last gift has been wrapped, I'm happy and comfortable and just a little bit turned on. Luke and I are packing up the remaining wrapping paper and ribbon when he nudges me.

"Uh-oh."

"What?" I follow the direction of his gaze to where Cara and Mila are talking with Dimi, casting the occasional glance in my direction. "Oh, you've got to be kidding. He's recruiting teenagers?"

Luke shakes his head. "I don't think he's the one doing the recruiting. Cara's been talking about how good it would be for Dom to date someone, and Mila loves the idea of romance. I bet they saw what Dimi and Sascha did, and now they've decided to put their own plans in action."

I have no idea how to respond to that, and before I can come up with something, the little huddle breaks up and Cara turns a determinedly cheerful smile on Dom.

"Ready to go, Dad? Oh, hey—we can give Mr. Jeffries a ride home, right? Dimi was just saying that he doesn't have his car here."

"Oh, she's good," Grant mutters as he sidles up beside me, smirking, then winks at me. "Watch this."

Raising his voice, he says, "No, we can take Oliver home. It's pretty much on our way."

"No!"

"No, we can't!"

Cara and Mila reply vehemently in unison. Jamie and the younger boys stare at them in befuddled shock. Derek smothers a laugh, and the rest of us—except Dimi, who looks like he's in pain—concentrate on anything other than the now red-faced teenage girls.

"I-I mean," Mila stutters, "there's no room in the car." She exchanges a relieved look with Cara.

"Good point," Derek says gravely, although his lips are twitching just a little bit. "Trav and I have room in the car. We can drop you off," he offers.

"Thank you," I say, and I don't know how I manage to keep a straight face. "That's really—"

"I have a better idea!" Cara declares brightly, drowning me out. "Why don't you come to our place, Mr. Jeffries, and keep Dad company tonight? I'm going out, and I'm sure Dad would rather eat dinner with you than alone." She shoots a pointed look at Dom. "After all, he doesn't often get the chance to hang out with his *friends*, and he and I were just saying how important *friends* are."

"What are we, then? He just spent the whole afternoon with us," Grant teases, and from the fulminating glare Mila sends his way, he's going to be on the receiving end of a teenage girl hissy fit later.

Dom steps in before one of the girls—or Dimi—has an aneurysm, raising a questioning brow at me. I nod slightly.

"Thanks, Cara, that's a great suggestion. It's a little

early still for dinner, but we'll drop Oliver off at home and he and I can make plans for later."

Immediately, both girls beam bright smiles at us. I'm a little disappointed in them—I thought they'd be able to keep their cool a little better than that.

"I feel like I have no idea what just happened," Jamie says. "Like, seriously, what did I miss?"

Apparently, this is my life now.

NINE

Dom

_____

When I was told that the town hosted a potluck party on Christmas Day for everyone who had nowhere else to go, I'm not really sure what I expected. I knew, of course, that the parks and resorts were open through the holidays, which means staff have to work. Even those who aren't rostered to work on Christmas Day might not find it worth the effort and expense of traveling to see family for just a few days. Joyville, remember, is populated mostly by people who work for Joy Universe and their immediate families—there are very few "native" Joyville residents.

Not everyone goes to the holiday party, I was assured. Many preferred to celebrate privately with small groups of friends, or not to celebrate at all. But for anyone who doesn't have other plans or wants lots of hoopla, the community center in Joyville throws open its doors with food, drink, company, and, I'm promised, a visit from Santa.

The town council—of which I am technically a member, although because I'm not elected, I don't actually get to vote on anything—informed me before Thanksgiving that if I was staying in town for the holidays, my attendance was mandatory. They didn't actually phrase it like that, but there was a lot of talk about being part of a community and showing respect for my employees and stuff like that, teamed with intense stares —and then Sascha Weston, who is technically *not* on the council but yet somehow has been at every meeting I've attended, patted my arm and assured everyone that *of course* I'd be there.

So I'm going to the holiday party.

And if Sascha Weston ever decides she wants a career in world domination, I'm crawling under my bed until the revolution is over.

Cara's actually excited about it—the party, not Sascha's revolution—although she's made me promise not to act like her dad. There are going to be a lot of kids from her school there, and only a few have been let in on the secret. I'm not sure how long she'll be able to keep it under wraps—there's bound to be someone today who'll recognize me from that night at the school. I made a promise, though, so we'll see how it goes.

Incidentally, Cara also suggested that we invite Oliver to come to the party with us "to keep from bringing two cars." There have been a lot of suggestions like this lately, along with ones to "save him from being/eating/going alone." She definitely hasn't given up on the idea of us dating, especially now that she's got Mila and Dimi and who knows who else egging her on. For the most part, I ignore it. Oliver and I have a good thing going, and I'm not prepared to expose it so the people of this town have more to gossip about.

Because, yes, they're still gossiping about us. The

initial furor died down when the news that we aren't dating got around, but it seems someone (my vote is on Dimi, though it could have been anyone) started a betting pool about whether we would go from "friends to lovers"—that's a direct quote—and if so, when. It seems that everyone at JU and in town is taking part in this pool, although oddly enough, nobody can tell me who's running it when I ask. Derek literally laughed in my face, but everyone else just shrugs and says they don't know.

Anyway, I gave in this once and told Cara she could invite Oliver to come with us, which thrilled her, but he'd already made plans to go with his friend Jaiden, who recently broke up with his long-term live-in boyfriend. Jaiden is staying with Oliver at the moment, which has limited our time together, but I can't be mad that he's choosing to support his heartbroken friend instead of fucking me.

Can I?

No. I can't. I'm just going to have to deal with it. Even if we were officially together, it would make me a total dick to be mad about this.

"Wow, look how many people are here already," Cara says as we turn into the parking lot. The party is apparently a very casual all-day thing, with people coming and going as they please, but she's right. I hadn't expected so many to be here from the beginning.

I park the car, and then we hop out and load up with our contributions to the food table. I also wrote a check last week for the organizing committee—aka Sascha Weston—to put toward drinks. This *is* a worthy community event, after all.

Inside is chaos. There's a stage at one end of the

room, and that appears to be where the "bar" is, but it looks like the food tables are being set up along the far wall. I say "looks like" because there are so many people milling about that it's hard to tell. And… is that Santa Claus? I thought his arrival would be a special event, but I guess he's just here all day.

I'm just about to suggest to Cara that we fight our way across the room and find somewhere to leave the food when Jason appears out of the crowd, smiling.

"Hi, Dom, Cara. So glad you came! Here, let me help you with that." He gestures into the crowd, and a moment later, two people I don't know come up and take the dishes from us. "We'll get them set up with the rest of the food. Did you remember the ingredient list?"

"They're taped to the lids, as requested," Cara assures him. She was very impressed by the requirement that all dishes be brought with a list of ingredients so allergens could be identified.

"Great! Help yourself to some drinks and have a wander around. Dimi's here somewhere. I just need to…" His gaze drifts over my shoulder, and with one last smile, he's gone.

"I think I see some people I know," Cara says. "See you, Dad!" And then she's gone too.

Time for a drink, and then I'll try to find someone to talk to.

I make it five steps before I'm stopped.

"Merry Christmas, Mr. Hurst!" A woman I don't know thrusts a candy cane at me.

"Uh, thank you," I manage, and she grins as she backs away.

Two more steps.

"Great to see you, sir!" two guys in their twenties

call, saluting me with their drinks. I wave back and smile.

"You too!" Does this happen to everyone, or is it another "director" thing?

I get my answer a moment later when an older couple melt out of the crowd to introduce themselves as "Tracey and John who own the pharmacy."

"It's lovely that you've come, Dominic. I can call you Dominic, can't I? The last director never bothered with any of the town events, but I knew from the moment they hired you that you'd be better than that."

"Uh, thank you, Tracey. I'm excited to be here." How the hell else am I supposed to respond to that? Sure, Ken, the director before me, seems to have only been interested in golf, to the detriment of the company and his career, but I'm not going to talk about him to other people, especially not people outside the JU corporate structure.

"Do you think you'll come to the New Year's fireworks next week? John and I would be glad to share a picnic with you."

"Dom, there you are!"

I'm saved from having to answer by the appearance of Trav, who slaps me on the shoulder in greeting before turning to my new nemesis, Tracey from the pharmacy.

"Hi, Tracey, John. Merry Christmas. I just need to borrow Dom for a second—Derek is looking for him. You know what these guys are like, never a day of rest." He smiles widely, grabs my arm, and tugs me into the crowd before Tracey can say anything else. I smile and wave at her so she doesn't decide we're being rude.

"Thanks for the rescue," I mutter, and Trav snorts.

"No thanks needed. I wasn't actually going to yank

you away like that, but then I heard her how-can-you-refuse invitation and figured you'd be okay with it. Remind me to tell you sometime how she and I met." We break through into a niche where Grant, Luke, and Dimi are gathered. "I saved him from a New Year's picnic with Tracey," Trav declares, and Grant's the only one who laughs.

"She's not so bad," he protests, and the others scoff.

"I've lived here almost my whole life," Dimi says, "and have known Tracey just as long. That's why I always take my prescriptions to the pharmacy in the Village, even though it costs more." His gaze flits over my shoulder, seemingly searching for something, and I bite the inside of my mouth to keep from smirking. "Did you come alone?"

"Oh, Cara's here somewhere," I say dismissively. "We're pretending not to know each other today."

"Yeah, but… you didn't bring anyone else?"

Grant jabs him in the side. "Give it a rest, Dimi."

"But—"

"I ran into your better half," I tell him. "He seemed to be all involved in the organizing. Shouldn't you be helping?"

For a second, I think he's going to persist, but finally he sighs and shakes his head. "Nope. Jase or Mom will likely find me later and rope me into cleaning up or something, but this is their gig. I'm just here to celebrate the day and be social."

As if on cue, someone passing calls a greeting to him, and he lifts a hand in response.

"Phew. I thought it was just me," I mutter.

"What was just you?" Luke asks.

I wave toward the crowd. "The whole people randomly saying hello thing."

"It is just you," Dimi informs me. "That was someone I went to school with. Random people don't say hello to me."

"The plight of being the director." Trav doesn't sound at all sympathetic, the prick. "Stick with us. Safety in numbers and all that."

"Because that makes me feel a lot better. Hey," I glance around, "where's Derek?"

For some reason, that sends Grant into peals of laughter. The others are all grinning broadly.

"What?" I've missed the joke.

"Did you see Santa as you came in?" Dimi asks, and I glance in that direction before looking back at him.

"Sure, but— No fucking way!" I whip around, craning to see over the crowd. Derek is Santa?

"Yep," Trav confirms. "Apparently he's a crowd favorite and does it nearly every year."

"Have you got pictures? Please tell me you have pictures."

Dimi rolls his eyes. "Did you not hear him say Derek does it nearly every year? There must be millions of pictures by now. It's impossible to embarrass him with them, though."

I shake my head. "I have newfound respect for Derek. And I'm also wondering if we should get him a psych evaluation. How long is he going to be doing that?" I look at Trav, who shrugs.

"Beats me. This is the first year I've been here for this."

"Most of the day," Dimi says. "The line will disappear later, and he'll be able to mingle, but he'll stay in costume all day for the kids who come later and want to meet him."

I frown. "That's a commitment. What's the hourly rate, and how many breaks does he get?"

Dimi stares at me like I'm speaking another language. "He gets as many breaks as he wants, whenever he wants them, and there's no hourly rate. It's a voluntary thing."

Well, that's not right. "Why?"

"Dom, it's a potluck event. The town donates use of the community center and pays for security and the cleaner who's going to come in tomorrow, as well as the turkeys and hams and the Santa gifts for the kids. The budget is stretched enough by that, which is why everyone is asked to bring food. All the organizers and helpers are volunteers, and so is Santa. That's how Derek ended up being Santa that first year—the guy who was going to do it decided at the last minute to visit his daughter for the holidays instead. Mom was nagging me to do it, and I bitched about it at work, and Derek volunteered."

"And Derek never thought to have the budget extended to allow for Santa to get paid?"

I get another weird look. "What's Derek got to do with the budget?"

A sinking feeling settles in my gut. "He's an AD. It's not his department, but given how relatively little it would cost, I'm sure events would have approved it if he asked." Come to think of it, I'm sure I saw Toby from events in the crowd before.

"Oh, I see where the confusion is," Grant interrupts as Dimi opens his mouth. "Dom, JU doesn't subsidize this party at all. The budget comes entirely from the town." He winces. "Uh, as I recall, when Derek found out about that, he asked Ken if JU could allocate some funds, but... Ken refused."

And here I'd been hoping I was wrong. "Who do I need to talk to about this? The town council? Your mom?" Jesus fucking Christ, most of the people here work for JU. The least the company can do is kick in some money to pay Santa and buy some food.

"Officially, the town council," Dimi says. "But Mom's been on the organizing committee for this party since I was a little kid, so you'll probably end up talking to her anyway."

"I'll find her later. And I'll talk to accounting when the office reopens." I'm really pissed off now. I mean, come on, Ken. It's bad enough he didn't notice his niece was running an embezzlement ring right under his nose. It's bad enough that he let the department heads run the company so he could play golf and stick his thumb up his own ass. But to refuse to pay for the town holiday party... that's just shit.

Suddenly, Dimi's face lights up, and in the next moment, a hand lands on my shoulder. "Merry Christmas," a familiar voice says, and all my anger and tension melts away. I turn and feast my eyes on Oliver's bright grin. "You're all looking awfully serious for being at a party. What are you talking about?"

"Dom's saving Christmas," Luke says, and I sputter like an idiot.

"I'm not... Jesus... Why would you say..." I give up and just shoot him a glare. "We were talking about work stuff," I tell Oliver, which is true enough. "You must be Jaiden," I add to the man standing beside him. "I'm Dominic Hurst."

"Nice to meet you," he says. He's smiling, but somehow he still looks like he's about to cry. I feel for the guy—breakups are hard.

Oliver quickly introduces Jaiden around the group, then says, "I hope you don't mind us crashing your circle. I figured it might stop people from trying to not-so-subtly interrogate me about Dom."

I groan. "Is it too early for a drink?"

"How bad is it?" Trav asks, and Oliver shrugs.

"It could be worse. Most of them manage to hint that they think we're secretly dating, but nobody's been too obnoxious."

"He's being kind," Jaiden interjects. "Unless somebody redefined 'obnoxious' and didn't tell me."

I meet Oliver's gaze and wonder how I can make this easier for him. It seems so unfair that he has to deal with this crap just for being—as everyone thinks—friends with me.

"You should just date," Dimi mutters. "Half the town already thinks you are. The other half wants you to."

I raise an eyebrow at him. "Did you seriously just tell us we should begin a romantic relationship because the town wants us to?"

He hesitates, and Trav pinches him. "Ow! Fine, no. That's not what I meant."

"I don't know you," Jaiden says solemnly, "but I don't believe you." He raises his hand for a high five. "I agree, they should definitely date."

Oliver looks at me. "I think we both need new friends."

"I'd take offense, but it's hard to argue given what we just heard," Luke says. "Let's go get something to drink, and then I should find Jordan and make sure he's still alive."

"He's fine," Grant says. "I saw him over there just a minute ago." He points into the crowd. "You know he'll die of embarrassment if you check up on him too often."

I let their conversation fade into the background as I lean toward Oliver. "It's good to see you," I murmur, and his teeth flash in a private kind of smile just for me.

"I haven't seen nearly enough of you lately," he replies, and I make a face.

"We'll have to make up for that. Too bad we can't sneak away now." I thought about it, but a single glance around put paid to that idea. There are so many eyes on us, so many people glancing our way and whispering to each other, that we'd never get away without being noticed—and wouldn't that be fuel for the gossips? Sneaking away from the holiday party together.

It would be fun, though.

"People would be waving us off." He chuckles. "But let's make plans for this week sometime—tomorrow?"

"Yes." Is that too eager? "Cara's home, but she won't mind if I go out."

"Great. Jaiden's going out of town for a few days, so we'll have the place to ourselves."

A thought strikes me. "While he's away, we should go to the restaurant I was telling you about at the Chateaux." I name one of the higher-end resorts at JU. "The place with the really great chocolate cake."

He nods, a smile lighting his face. "That sounds amazing. I've been wanting to go ever since you mentioned it—seven-layer chocolate fudge cake? I can't pass that up. But will we be able to get a table for tomorrow?"

"Maybe not tomorrow," I concede. I don't like to throw my influence around too much for things like restaurant reservations. "But the day after, sure." I'm about to add that he'll love the appetizer grazing platter when I become aware that our friends have stopped talking. We glance up and find them staring at us. All of them.

It's a bit disconcerting.

"What?" I ask.

Grant shakes his head. "Nothing," he declares. "Drinks. Um, we've been talking about getting some for ages, but we keep getting distracted."

He's right. "Let's go, then."

The group starts to drift in the general direction of the bar, and I fall into step beside Oliver—only to have Luke grab my arm. Oliver looks over his shoulder questioningly.

"I just need to pick his brain about something," Luke says cheerfully. "You know us business types—a day off is a day wasted."

Oliver smiles and turns back, and I raise an eyebrow at Luke. "A day off is a day wasted?"

He shrugs. "It just came to me. Don't be a hater. What the hell are you doing?"

I blink. "What do you mean?"

His expression turns cautious. "I thought you and Oliver were friends with bennies?"

"We are."

He groans and rubs the bridge of his nose. "Okay, so I don't have a lot of experience with that kind of thing, since I was with the same guy for fifteen years before I met Grant, but the way I understand it, you're supposed to be people who hang out casually and also have sex."

"Yes. That's right. And that's what we are."

"Dom… you just made a date with him. Two, actually. At least one of which at a time when your daughter is home. Do you remember saying you didn't want a relationship because it would take away from the time you could spend with Cara?"

I…

Fuck.

"And," he continues, "if the place with the chocolate cake is the one I think it is, your very public date is going to be at a very romantic restaurant."

"I went there for a business lunch—with *you*," I protest, but he shakes his head.

"We went there when it was *closed* because it's in Derek's district and the chef and the resort manager wanted more opinions on the new menu. That place doesn't open for lunch."

Fuck. Am I really that stupid and unobservant?

"I was distracted by the food," I mutter. And also, I remember thinking how intimate the place was, and what a great prelude to seduction eating there would be.

I really am that stupid.

"Okay, let's do a quick assessment," Luke says, the business consultant in him rearing its head. "How many times a week do you talk to Oliver on the phone without anything sexual happening? On average."

I think about it. "Maybe three." If you count sex, then we talk every day, but I'm not telling Luke that.

"And texting?"

I sigh. "Every day. Fine, I see what you're getting at."

"Do you? Because from where I'm standing, he's your secret boyfriend."

"Fuck, never say that again." I shudder. "It sounds like something from a trashy teen movie."

He laughs. "God, it does, doesn't it? Dom... look. We all understand why you chose not to start a relationship, but it seems like you're in one anyway. And if you want to continue to keep it quiet, we'll all do our best to support you. But the town's already gossiping anyway, so maybe that's something you want to think about. It would be a lot easier to spend time together if you didn't have to sneak around."

I stare at him for a long moment. He's right, of course, but...

"Let's get those drinks."

TEN

Oliver

_____

It's a huge relief when the doorbell rings. Dom said he was coming, but he was acting so weird yesterday at the holiday party that I started to wonder if maybe he'd changed his mind. I don't know what happened— one second he was his usual self and we were making plans, and then the next he was being all… jittery.

I open the door and let him in, and sure enough, he's still got that weird look on his face.

"Hey." I make sure the door is closed, then lean in to kiss him, but he takes a step back, eyes going wide.

"We need to talk," he blurts. "Now."

Oh-kay… I wave him over to the couch and go sit beside him. "Is something wrong? Is Cara okay?"

"Cara's fine. She's at home. Watching TV. Doing nothing, really."

"Sounds like she's having a lazy day." Does that worry him? I mean, the kid's entitled to an occasional TV day. She gets good grades and stays out of trouble. I know he's driven and ambitious, but this seems a little overkill.

"Yeah, but what I mean is… I could have spent the day with her."

Oh. "You didn't have to come over," I say, being careful not to let my sudden hurt show in my voice. "If you wanted to spend today with Cara, I—"

"No, no. Fuck, I'm doing this wrong." He runs his hands through his hair, something I've noticed he does only when he's particularly stressed. "What I mean is, I knew Cara would be home today, but I still made plans to see you. Because I wanted to be with you. And… when I think about our… us, it strikes me that we're more than just friends."

That was not what I was expecting to hear. My jaw drops, and I gather myself to refute what he's just said—

And stop.

Because he's right.

I can't believe I've been so willfully blind to it. We're not just friends who get each other off anymore—we're in a relationship.

I wish he was with me when I wake up.

We text throughout the day about trivial stuff.

We talk all the time—I can't go to sleep without having spoken to him. Even when we've both had long days and are too tired for phone sex, *we still talk*.

And we hang out. Not just for sex, but movies and meals and… hell, a few weeks back, we binged six episodes of one of my favorite telenovelas.

"How did this happen?" I ask faintly, and he shrugs.

"I guess we're just too comfortable with each other. The question is… what do we do now?"

I look up sharply. "What do you mean? Do we have to *do* anything?"

"No." He raises his hands. "We can just leave things

as they are, if you want. But, honestly, I don't know how much longer we'll be happy this way. I know I already... miss you all the time. I get frustrated when we're not able to see each other."

My insides get all warm and melty. "Me too," I admit, then I sigh. "Wow, so much for neither of us wanting a relationship."

He leans over and kisses my neck, then rests his head on my shoulder. "I've been stressing about this since yesterday," he confesses, "but now that I've told you, being here... I feel so much better. Yet the problem hasn't gone away."

I lean my head against his, understanding exactly what he means. I feel better with him here too. Sharing.

We just sit for a moment, enjoying each other's nearness. Finally, I say, "How do you want to handle this? Do you still want to keep it quiet—other than Cara and our close friends, I mean. Or do you want to go completely public?"

He straightens and turns his body toward me, his gaze serious. "It's up to you. Your original reason for not wanting a relationship with me was that you didn't want to be dating 'the director.'" He actually makes air quotes, which strikes me as absolutely adorable for some reason, and I bite back a smile. "That hasn't changed. You'll probably cop the brunt of the gossip. So this next step is up to you."

I lean back against the couch, absently reaching out to take his hand while I think about it. He's right. Nothing has changed in that regard from when we started this a couple months ago. I would still be dating the highest-profile man in town, the man on whom the whole town depends. There would be gossip. There would be a spotlight on me, where in the past I've tried to keep my personal life to myself.

But I'd be able to date Dom publicly. No more sneaking around, stealing time when Cara's out. We could go to restaurants together and not have to worry about casual touching. We could go to the New Year's Eve fireworks picnic and snuggle under a blanket together.

The question is whether or not I consider this something that's going to last. Because long-term, I am absolutely not going to be happy snatching moments with Dom when people aren't paying attention and pretending to only be his friend in public. Eventually, we would have to own up to being together.

I squeeze his hand and lift it to my lips for a kiss. "Let's go tell Cara now. And then tomorrow we can go out to dinner and kiss in public."

His face lights up in a grin. "Yeah, that's one way to share the news. Are you sure?"

"Yes. Absolutely." Part of me is lighter just having made the decision, and I love seeing how happy he is.

He kisses me, and I can feel his smile against my mouth, which makes me smile, and we're kissing and smiling and one thing leads to another.

It's several hours before we go talk to Cara.

"*WHAT?*" The dropped-jaw expression on Cara's face makes me want to laugh. "You've been together all this time and kept it a *secret*?" She says "secret" like it's a dirty word, and Dom winces.

"Surprise?"

That's the wrong thing for him to say.

"Seriously, Dad, when are you going to stop treating me like a little kid? Why was it such a big secret for you to be dating someone? I've been actively trying to get you to do this exact thing… with this exact person!" She flings a hand in my direction, and I really don't envy Dom at this moment. I doubt he wants to tell his seventeen-year-old daughter that we were having no-strings sex.

"I didn't tell you because we haven't been officially dating. We were just friends. And then when we realized something more was going on, we kept it quiet while we decided if that was something we wanted to explore. There are parts of my life I'm not always going to share, Cara. Oliver and I knew that you liked the idea of us together, and we didn't want to get your hopes up in case it didn't work out that way." He keeps his tone even and reasonable, somehow walking that fine line of being her parent without treating her like a child.

She sighs, then comes to hug him. "I'm happy for you both." I get a hug next, much to my surprise. "Are you going to keep it quiet, or…?"

Dom shakes his head. "We've decided to go public. You're the first to know, of course."

Her eyes widen. "Oh, please let me be the one to tell Dimi!"

A laugh bursts out of me. "I forgot we'd have to tell Dimi," I admit.

"Pleeeeeease," Cara begs, dancing around with her hands clasped together. "Please please pleeeeeeeease?"

Dom looks at me, eyebrow raised, and I just grin and nod. "Fine."

"Yessss! Give me your phone; I'm calling him now."

She snatches her father's phone from his hand and disappears down the hall toward the bedrooms.

"That went well," I say, tongue in cheek.

Dom snorts. "We don't have to worry about how to go public. The whole town will know within a couple hours." He closes the two feet between us and drapes his forearms over my shoulders. "As soon as I get my phone back, let's go back to your place. Or..." He meets my gaze steadily. "I want to spend the night with you, but I'm not comfortable leaving Cara alone overnight. Would you maybe stay here? All night, I mean."

My heartbeat picks up speed. It's silly, really. We've had sex more times than I can easily count, spent hours in each other's company. I've even spent the night here before, when Cara was sleeping at a friend's place. But staying over while she's here, as Dom's official boyfriend... that makes my breath catch and butterflies erupt in my stomach.

"If Cara doesn't mind," I reply, and my voice is a little unsteady.

"If I don't mind what?" she asks, and we both turn our heads to look at her, but neither of us moves back.

I like this.

"Oliver staying over tonight," Dom says, and she shrugs.

"Sure, I don't mind. Dimi wants to talk to you, Dad." She holds out the phone. "Can we get takeout for dinner? I thought about cooking a celebratory meal, but we can do that when I've had more time to plan. We're running kind of low on groceries."

Does nothing faze this kid?

"Takeout's fine," Dom says, taking the phone from

her. "I'll just be a sec," he tells me, and a second later he's saying hello and walking toward the hallway.

Leaving me with Cara.

Who tips her head to one side, studying me, and smiles.

"I really am glad about this, you know," she says. "I think you and Dad are gonna be great for each other. So you don't have to worry about any teenage angst from me over my dad dating someone new."

"Thank you." Honesty compels me to add, "Your dad and I both thought you'd be okay with it. Your maturity is something he's so proud of."

Her smile turns a little shy, and I'm reminded of how young she is. "He's a good dad—mostly, anyway." She rolls her eyes. "Are you guys ready for the roller coaster of crap that's going to come your way? There are a lot of people talking about you already, and you're just 'friends.'" She makes air quotes just like her dad did earlier, and I have to bite my lip to keep from smiling.

"We're not looking forward to it, but we're prepared." I make a face. "I should probably expect to have a conversation with the principal once school starts again." Darryn's an avid gossip hound and has tried several times to subtly feel me out about my friendship with Dom.

Concern crosses Cara's face. "It's not going to be a problem, is it? You dating the director and me being a student at the school?" Her jaw sets. "They can't dictate who you can and can't date—"

"Relax," I interrupt before she gets all worked up. "You're not in any of my classes, so there's no problem with me dating your dad. As far as him being the director"—I shrug—"it's not a problem except for the attention it will bring. There might be some disruption amongst the students, so we'll have a plan in place." I level a steady look at her. "What about you? The more attention on your dad, the more likely it is other students will realize you're his daughter."

She makes a wrist-twisting gesture that I interpret as "I know." "I guess I'm ready for it to come out," she admits. "I won't enjoy it, but I know who my friends are now, and they already know. Whatever the rest think doesn't really matter. There's only a semester left, anyway."

"Your dad said your first choice for college is Princeton?"

"Mmm, yeah." She nods. "It's a good school, and I like the idea of staying on the East Coast. My next pick is Stanford, but that's a long way."

Dom comes back in, grinning and shaking his head. "Well, Dimi's going to activate his phone tree or whatever, so we can expect the news to be all over town within the hour."

A tingle of excitement runs through me. For better or worse, Dom's now officially my boyfriend.

OVER THE NEXT TWO WEEKS, I learn the price of fame.

I've lived in Joyville for ten years and taught at Joyville High that whole time. Being a teacher in a smaller community means you get to know a lot of people—or rather, they know you. The students at the school, usually their parents, anybody they introduce you to when you happen to run into them at the store or the gas station. I have neighbors and friends too. It's not that I was a complete recluse or that nobody knew who I was.

But now, everybody knows who I am.

It's not just whispering and pointing anymore, or people I know trying to maneuver information out of me. Complete strangers are coming up to me in the streets and asking for favors.

Yes. Favors.

They want me to use my "influence" to get Dom to do things. Things they think need to change at JU. Jobs they think should go to their spouses/kids. Scholarships JU should award.

That last one confused me, because I happen to know that JU already awards five college scholarships for local students. Tuition fully paid, and a stipend for living expenses, to a college of their choice within the US. It's something that was set up decades ago, and I encourage all of my students who are interested in going to college to apply. I explained this, of course, to the man who accosted me outside the pharmacy, but he insisted that his kid shouldn't have to go through the application process, that she was so "special and talented" that Dom should create a new scholarship especially for her.

What was I supposed to say to that? I never would have thought I'd be glad to be hailed by Tracey, who owns the pharmacy with her husband, but I was. It gave me the excuse I needed to bail out of that conversation.

When I asked Dom how he copes with all that, he was genuinely shocked. Our best guess is that people see me as a safe intermediary between them and "the director," and ask me things they're not willing to take to him personally.

On the plus side, I've gained a new friend in Dom's assistant, Layla. I actually knew her already, although just casually, since I've taught three of her children and will likely teach the fourth in the next few years. She called me the first day Dom was back at the office after the break to assure me that she was thrilled we'd gotten together and that she was the person to call if I ever needed Dom's work schedule rearranged. I mean, I'd never do that without talking to him first, but it's nice to know I've got contacts on the inside, so to speak.

And the part that makes all the crap worth it? I get to spend so much more time with Dom now. Most evenings, I go to his place so we can eat with Cara. We watch TV together, make out on the couch (if Cara's not watching with us), and just generally enjoy each other. We've gone out a few times as well, and even though we're not doing anything so different from before, it's completely different.

I'm enjoying a Dom-induced daydream in the teachers' lounge during my lunch break when Jaiden collapses into a chair next to me and ruins it. He's doing a lot better now than he was, but he's still not his usual self. Having the guy you were sure was "the one" dump you and kick you out isn't easy to get over. He's been looking at getting his own place, though I told him he's welcome to stay with me as long as he needs.

I've been so used to seeing a glum expression on his face that his wicked grin is a big shock, and I do a double take.

"You look… happy." It's not exactly right, but I'm not going to say he looks smug.

"Oh, I am. I confiscated something during my last class that makes me so, so happy."

Shock overtakes me. "Jaiden!" I hiss, looking around to make sure nobody heard. "You can't do that. It needs to be reported and destroyed."

For a second, he looks confused, but then he starts to laugh so hard I'm not sure he can breathe. "Not… drugs…," he wheezes. "Holy crap, Oliver, how could you think—" He dissolves into more laughter, and now that I'm reassured that he's not high on school property during school hours, I patiently wait him out. I smile politely at some of our colleagues who are clearly wondering what's wrong with him.

"Shoo," he says finally, wiping tears from his eyes. "I really needed that. I can't remember the last time I laughed so hard."

"I'm so glad to have helped. Are you ready to share now?"

He slumps back in his seat and flips open the folder he brought with him—probably from his last class. "Here." He passes me a sheet of paper.

One glance is enough to horrify me.

"Oh my god," I whisper. "You confiscated this from a *student*?"

It's a homemade flyer, clearly printed either in the lab here at the school or at someone's home, with the heading VOTE FOR YOUR FAVORITE SILVER FOX and four color photos labeled A-D. One is of me, taken from last year's yearbook. The other three are George Clooney, Mark Harmon, and Anderson Cooper. There's a tally of pen marks under each picture, along with a bunch of comments. The worst one says, *only Mr J has what it takes to catch a milyonair.*

Which is disturbing on many levels, not least of which is the spelling.

Jaiden's still grinning, and now he nods as he unwraps the sandwich he brought from home. "Yes. And as you can see, it had circulated through nearly the whole class before I noticed it."

I stare at the sheet. "How can you find this funny, Jaiden?" I can't believe the students are *this* interested in my love life. They're not supposed to think I even have one!

"Oh, relax. It's harmless. They do this with celebrities all the time."

"But I'm not a celebrity," I argue. "I'm a teacher at this school who sees them every day and has to teach them."

He puts down the sandwich. "Have you been having problems in class?"

"Well… no." Aside from some initial whispers and giggling when the news first broke, my students haven't been behaving any differently.

He shrugs. "Then it's not a problem. They've put your personal life into the celebrity category. As long as there's no crossover between that and your professional life, you'll be fine."

I'm sure it's not that simple, but it's not like there's anything I can do. It would be extremely difficult to find out who this little survey originated with, and the process of trying would just attract a lot of attention.

I sigh, then crumple the sheet, preparing to throw it away.

"Hey!" Jaiden yelps, grabbing for it. "That's mine!"

"Are you joking?" He can't be serious.

"No. I'm keeping it to cheer me up when I'm having a bad day. You know, say what you will about these kids, they've got great taste in men."

I groan.

It's three relatively peaceful days before the next distur-
bance. Dom and I went out for dinner at the noodle
place in town last night, so when the whispering began
again this morning, I assumed it was because of that.
Although why anyone would find us eating dinner interesting, I have no idea.

Anyway, I ignore it as I have been. The students
have been respectful of my privacy to my face, and I
don't want to know what's going on behind my back.
My fellow teachers have advised that there's been some
chatter in other classrooms and that the students were
reminded that they should mind their own business and
concentrate on their studies.

And then…

"Mr. Jeffries?"

I turn from wiping the whiteboard and smile politely
at two senior girls who are in none of my classes—Jacey
and Lauren. I've taught them both in the past, and while
they're decent students, their concentration is more on
classroom politics than their studies. "Yes?"

They exchange glances, and Lauren twirls a lock of
hair around a finger in a way that seems decidedly
nervous. It's Jacey who speaks.

"Uh, we had a question…"

I keep the smile on my face. "About one of your
classes? Or the English department?"

She shakes her head. Lauren's face is going pink.
"No, uh, it's about another student."

My smile disappears, but I make sure to keep my

face calm and encouraging. I'm not so naïve as to think we don't have any bullying at this school, but we have some strict anti-bullying policies, and all faculty members attend regular training on dealing with bullies and bullied students. We encourage victims of bullying to come forward for support. Still, I'd be a little surprised if that's what this is about—these girls are part of a well-established and popular clique.

"Is someone making things difficult for you?" I ask gently. A lot of bullied students don't acknowledge that they're actually being bullied. They see it as teasing or a group dynamic. An initial change in terminology often makes it easier for them to admit there's actually a prob-lem, and then the awareness of it being bullying comes later.

Lauren shakes her head. "Nothing like that, Mr. Jeffries," she assures me, and I smile again.

"That's good." Although it leaves me wondering what this could be about. Have they noticed another student being bullied?

"But we wondered if you would know…"

I hold on to my patience.

"Is it true that Cara Hurst is the director's daughter?"

Oh. Oh, *hell*. Poor Cara.

I level a steady look at both girls. "Are you gossiping about a classmate?"

They both shake their heads. "She's not in any of our classes," Lauren says. "Not since she left Mrs. Hamilton's class."

Are they serious? For a split second, I wonder if I should pull them up for that—I mean, talk about semantics—but decide not to bother.

"I'm sure you both have better things to do than gossip about anyone at this school—I know I do. Is it your lunch now?"

It looks like Jacey's going to argue, her jaw setting stubbornly, but then she concedes defeat. "Yes."

"You'd better go eat, then."

Thankfully, they do, leaving me to ponder their audacity and what I should do next. Does Cara know the student body is talking? If not, she deserves some warning… but if I pull her aside, that will just make things worse.

In the end, I text Dom.

Oliver: Bad news. There're rumors that Cara is your daughter. I don't know if she knows—can you warn her?

I head to the front office to give Darryn a heads-up. I'm not sure who Cara's homeroom teacher is, but he'll know. I guess all her teachers will need to be advised to be on the lookout for any trouble.

Poor kid.

My phone chirps just as I pass Maria's desk.

Dom: Just texted now. Thanks for letting me know. Do I need to come down there?

Oliver: I don't think so. See what Cara says. I'm going to have a chat with Darryn now.

Dom: Darryn?

Oliver: The principal.

I get a thumbs-up in return, then knock on Darryn's door. His call is muffled, but clear enough for me to enter.

"Oliver, hi." He smiles, but it disappears when he sees my face. "Oh, crap. What's happened?"

I close the door behind me and take a seat in one of the visitor chairs. "It's not bad. More of an FYI. Two of the seniors just asked me if Cara is Dom's daughter."

He sighs and grabs a pen. "I'll make sure the faculty all knows. Is Cara aware?"

I shrug. "I asked Dom to text her but haven't heard back yet. She knew this was a possibility, especially now. I think she's more comfortable with it happening this semester than last."

"She's found her feet here now," Darryn agrees. "Who were the students?" I tell him, and he pulls a face. "They've both had a few warnings for stuff like this. Not overt bullying, nothing we can really action, but whispers and giggles that seem to make others uncomfortable."

"Yeah, the problem with bullying is how hard some of it is to define and prove," I say sourly. "If two students are talking between themselves only while seeming to stare at another student and laughing, it's hard to call them out for bullying, but the effect on the third student can still be harsh." My phone chimes, and I glance at it.

Dom: Cara says she's heard the rumors but is ignoring them for now. Her friends are apparently stepping up too, but I'm not sure in what way.

I relay the information to Darryn while texting an acknowledgment.

"We'll keep an eye on the situation." He sighs again. "In the meantime, how are you doing? Are things settling down?"

"Relatively. It seems to be getting better, anyway. I wish it wasn't an issue at all," I admit. Being with Dom is amazing, but being with the director? Not so much.

Proof of that is that Darryn and I are having this conversation.

"I wish that for you too," he says. "Make sure you let me know if there are any problems I can deal with."

I smile and thank him, but the truth is, there's nothing he can do to lessen the impact of Dom's job in this town.

ELEVEN

Dom

—————

"Dad, Oliver, come *on*," Cara yells. "If I'd known you were going to take this long, I would've gotten a lift with my friends!"

I finish tying my sneakers while Oliver leans against the bedroom door laughing silently.

"I'm not wrong, am I?" I ask him dryly. "She was the one who insisted we had plenty of time and should watch that YouTube video, right? Even though I told her I wanted to have a shower before we left?"

He nods. "I don't think it matters, though."

I get up as he opens the door and follow him down the hall to where Cara's waiting impatiently by the front door.

"Finally!" she exclaims. "I don't even want to know what you were doing in there."

Oh my god.

"I was having a shower, Cara," I declare, grabbing my jacket from her.

"Sure, right," she mutters. "A shower."

I stop dead halfway through the door and am about

to ask her *exactly* what her problem is, but Oliver grabs my arm and yanks me forward.

"Come on," he says determinedly. "We're ready now. Let's not dawdle and risk missing the fireworks." He wrangles us down to the garage and into my car, and by the time we're on the road, Cara seems to be over her snit.

"Are you sure it's going to be good?" she asks me for what feels like the billionth time. "It's not going to be hokey and racist, is it?"

I glance at her in the rearview mirror. "Like I said before, planning for the entire event has been overseen by the Chinese community in Joyville. It's not especially big, but we had a lot of participants, and they didn't seem afraid to express their opinions. We also brought in a planning consultant who is known for organizing Chinese New Year celebrations. Ms. Huang was very strict with the events department. The celebrations should be respectful and fun."

Cara nods. "Okay."

I understand her concern—it was one I had myself five months ago when I found out the events department and Derek's team were planning a Chinese New Year celebration at Planet Joy, our flagship theme park. I definitely didn't want JU culturally appropriating the holiday and screwing it up. Derek and Toby had things well in hand, however, and had already consulted our local Chinese community—who were pleased at the idea of a large-scale celebration—and hired Lin Huang, who has an impeccable track record. In fact, based on her association with the event, we were able to attract a lot of Chinese Americans to JU for this week, some in big family groups.

So the event should be a success on all levels. Of course, that doesn't mean I'm not worried.

I skip the staff parking lot and drive around to the back entrance of the park, where my swipe card gains me access to the small private lot for the park manager and visitors from the admin building. Most of the spots are taken, but one has been left for me.

"This is a nice perk," Oliver says dryly. "I'm guessing there won't be any lining up for admission, either?"

Cara gasps. "That's so gross," she says. "It's bad enough we're not paying for tickets."

I turn off the car and turn to give her a level look. "Annual park passes are included in the benefits package for all employees. Any children of staff under sixteen are free. You, my dear pain in the ass, are not sixteen anymore, so I paid to purchase your annual pass when you moved down here—as I did Oliver's pass for tonight. Yes, I got a staff discount. No, it was not more than any other employee's. If you want to take your pass, go around to the front of the park, and line up, you're more than welcome to. I, however, work a minimum of sixty hours a week in this job, many of them after you're sleeping peacefully at night, and I'm not ashamed to take advantage of the perks that gives me. Okay?"

She grimaces. "Sorry, Dad. I know you work hard and deserve those perks."

I nod but don't say anything else as we all get out of the car. I love Cara, but I'm not going to let anyone make me feel bad about myself.

We enter through the side staff gate, scanning our passes. Normally I'd scan through with my employee swipe, but since I'm not officially working tonight, I use my annual pass instead. It actually does make a difference for legal purposes, especially in the event of an evacuation. Once we're in, I raise a brow at Cara.

"I guess you want to go find your friends."

She rises on tiptoe and kisses my cheek. "I'll come find you for the fireworks at midnight." Then she heads off into the crowd.

"Keep your phone on you!" I shout after her, and she waves in acknowledgment without turning around. I turn back to Oliver and hold out my hand. "Let's check it out."

Hand in hand, we wander through the park. I'm impressed by the work that's been done for this week's event, and especially for tonight. There's a plethora of red decorations—banners, bunting, and flags are just the beginning—and red lanterns hung everywhere, and the sound of drums fades in and out depending on where we are. I know that there are dragon and lion dances being performed at semiregular intervals throughout the park, and it doesn't take too long for us to stumble upon one. I've seen it before, but it's still remarkable to watch.

We stop a few times to get snacks and drinks, and of course we run into people we know—or who know us. The evening is clear and cold, but there's no wind, and the press of the crowd helps to keep the chill away.

"Did you want to go on any of the rides?" I think to ask at one point, and Oliver laughs.

"Not tonight. Another time, maybe." He smiles at me, and I swear, my heart squeezes. I didn't even know I wanted this in my life, but now I can't bear to think of not having it.

After a few hours, the crowd changes slightly, with

the younger families heading out to put their sleepy children to bed and the post-dinner and theater people swarming in for fun and fireworks. My phone vibrates in my pocket with a text from Luke, advising me that they've staked out a spot on the lawn in front of Joy Bear's Interplanetary Headquarters. Oliver and I begin moving in that direction, but we're in no rush. There's plenty of time before the fireworks still, and I've been assured that there's a good view of them from almost everywhere in the park.

It's harder than I thought to find our friends. The lawn is covered with people hunkered down with blankets and snacks and hot drinks, waiting for the fireworks to ring in the New Year. The park is rarely open this late —the solar New Year is the only other time. We pick our way carefully through the encampments, looking for our group. Oliver's the one who finally catches sight of Dimi waving.

They're sprawled over two picnic blankets, and only two groups beyond them is Cara with Mila and an assortment of their friends. My daughter waves, and I wave back as we stake a claim on one corner of a blanket.

"Well?" I ask Derek. "Are we happy?"

He grins broadly. "We're ecstatic. The feedback so far has been exceptional. Toby and I got kicked out of the park manager's office hours ago because we weren't needed."

"That's what I like to hear." I look around. "We've been enjoying it. Lin and your teams have done a great job."

Grant leans forward. "Did you get any food?"

Oliver nods enthusiastically. "I could have kept eating all night."

"You're not the only one who's said that," Derek muses, and he and Grant exchange glances.

"Possibly something to explore as an alternative to the standard park fast food?" Grant pulls out his phone and taps away at the screen, presumably making a note. I smile but say nothing.

Oliver leans against my side, and I wrap my arm around him and rest my head against his. Maybe I shouldn't be quite so demonstrative in public—after all, technically this is my workplace and I am the boss—but I'm not working tonight, the lighting is muted, and I really, truly don't want to let him go.

We talk quietly amongst ourselves, huddled together to chase away the chill of the night, waiting for the fireworks. There's a vendor nearby selling hot drinks, but although we discuss getting some, none of us can quite be bothered to get up. Are we getting old?

Oliver and Jason laugh outright when Luke poses the question.

"You've got some time left," Jason tells him dryly, then winks. "I say we make Dimi get the drinks. He's the youngest."

Dimi protests vociferously, then stops midsentence and says, "Am I arguing about the fact that you just called me young?"

We're all snickering when a long shadow looms over us.

"You're all kind of pathetic," Mila announces in a typical fifteen-year-old manner. "We can hear you complaining about how old you are from over there." She gestures over her shoulder. I glance that way and am rewarded by smiles and waves from the group of high schoolers, including Cara. "However," she continues, "I have a solution for you."

"A solution to being old?" Grant asks, sitting up straighter. "Honey, you should patent that real quick."

She rolls her eyes. "No. A solution to not wanting to get up." She holds out her hand, palm up, and wriggles her fingers. "I'll get your drinks—if you pay for ours too."

Luke groans, but I laugh and pull out my annual pass, which is linked to my credit card for charges within the parks. "That sounds like a sweet deal to me. If you're hungry, get some snacks too." I hand her the card.

She grins and tosses her hair. "Nah, drinks will be fine. Wouldn't want to take advantage." She waves at the others in her group, and Cara and two others get up and join her as she heads for the vendor.

"You don't have to pay—"

I wave my hand, cutting off Luke's protest. "Please. That was fun. And anyway, if Cara had thought about it, she could have just used her pass—or Mila could have used hers?" I raise an eyebrow at him, and he nods. "So it was more about wanting to get one over on us than the money. I'll bet she enjoyed calling us old and pathetic."

He squeezes his eyes shut, then chuckles. "She would have loved it."

Sooner than I would have thought, given the line and the number of drinks we needed, we're all warming our hands around paper cups and sipping hot liquid.

"Mmm, that's nice," Oliver murmurs beside me, and

then a moment later, a thrill of excitement runs through the crowd. "Oh, they must be about to start."

The first explosion of color comes only seconds later, followed by an "Ooooooh!" from thousands of mouths. I turn to grin at Oliver, only to find him grinning back at me. Bright colors cast by the fireworks play over his face, chased by shadows, and I can't resist leaning in for a kiss.

This is everything I never knew I wanted and everything I'll keep for the rest of my life.

TWELVE

Oliver
_____

My concentration in the weekly staff meeting is a little shaky. Admittedly, the agenda this week isn't terribly exciting—it's all just routine, and those of us who've been here for years aren't hearing anything new. My mind is elsewhere, occupied by thoughts of Dom and the weekend getaway we've been talking about having when Cara goes to visit her grandparents next month. We could lock ourselves in and spend the whole weekend naked, but the idea of frolicking naked at a private villa or something at a tropical resort is equally appealing. Maybe I'll get some travel brochures and look into it.

I huff a tiny snort to myself. When I mentioned brochures the other night, Cara rolled her eyes and told me not to contribute to the needless massacre of trees. "The information you need is all online," she pointed out, "and it's not like you're not comfortable with technology." She's right, of course, but there's just something about print brochures. It's definitely a hangover from the old days, because an online search *would* be more convenient.

"Oliver?" Darryn says, and from his tone, it's not the first time.

"Sorry." I wince. "Could you repeat that, please?"

Lindy, one of the math teachers, snickers. "Counting the minutes until you can get home to your man?" she teases, and half the room breaks into laughter.

"It's so good to see you distracted like this," Marisa, the head of the art department, adds. "You've always been such a perfect, professional ideal of a teacher, and now we know you're also a guy who daydreams about his hot boyfriend." I can feel my cheeks getting hot and am glad for my beard. Marisa and Lindy are both lovely, and we've been friendly for years, so I know this is in good fun, but I never thought to have my love life discussed at a staff meeting.

"Although," she continues thoughtfully, "I never would have picked him to be your type. If someone had asked, I would have said you'd go for an academic, not a business type like the director."

There's a round of agreeing and disagreeing noises —who would have thought so many of my colleagues had thought about my ideal partner?—and one very clear "*What?*"

I glance down the table at Edith, who has a pinched expression on her face. Clearly she doesn't think this is an appropriate conversation, and she's not exactly wrong. Darryn must agree, because he clears his throat and says, "What I asked, Oliver, is whether you plan to have an overnight field trip at the school this semester. You said the last one was very successful?"

Oh, right. "Yes on both counts. We noticed a better

quality of engagement in the assignments that were turned in for that book, and the participation level among the students who weren't required to attend was higher than we expected. I think it's definitely worth doing again."

He makes a note. "Okay. I'll be sure to mention that at the board meeting tomorrow night—it got quite a bit of positive attention last time."

Beside me, Jaiden snorts softly. "Given the old sticks on the board, that's surprising."

The meeting shuffles on for another fifteen minutes before Darryn lets us go. It ran a little longer than usual. That sometimes happens before the monthly school board meeting—Darryn likes to make sure all his *i*'s are dotted and *t*'s are crossed beforehand, even though we've never really had any issues with the board since I've been working here.

"What are you doing tonight?" I ask Jaiden as we head out to the staff parking lot.

He shrugs. "Dinner. Grading. Netflix. Nothing terribly interesting. You?"

"The same. Want to come round for dinner?"

He shoots me a sideways look. "And be the third wheel? Nope."

I scoff. "Dom's got a late meeting, and I've got a pile of grading to do, so I'm not seeing him tonight, thanks very much. If you want to eat alone—"

"Okay, fine, sorry." He's grinning. "I'll come over. Wouldn't want you to have to deal with the echoing emptiness of your house now that you're so used to having someone there all the time."

I'm highly tempted to shove him and take back the invitation, but the truth is, he's not wrong. I spend so much time with Dom these days that my house does feel empty when it's just me. Plus, I don't get to spend as much time with Jaiden outside school anymore, and he's only teasing.

"Just for that, you're buying dinner." I smirk at him as I reach my car. "I think we'll order from the place that has the really expensive dumplings." He's laughing as I get in, and if we weren't on school property, I'd be tempted to flip him the bird, but I know there are likely to still be students around here somewhere—and knowing my luck, they'd appear just in time to see me.

———

Toward the end of third period the next day, Darryn appears in my classroom doorway, face pale. My students are in the midst of a heated discussion about the Oxford comma, which I admit I started just to entertain myself—who would have thought a roomful of sixteen-year-olds could get heated about commas?—and I'm basically just letting them run through the last few minutes before the bell. So I keep one eye and ear on them and go over to see what's bothering Darryn.

"I just got a call from the board," he mutters urgently, and I'm momentarily amused by an image of a boardroom table calling him. "They want you at the meeting tonight."

What? "Me? Why?" Is this something to do with the overnight field trip?

"I don't know, exactly. Something about a complaint they want to discuss with you. I asked but couldn't get more information."

"A *complaint*?" I'm surprised. Oh, not because someone's complained about me—that happens to teachers far more often than you'd think. There's always a parent who believes their darling child has been treated unfairly. Those sorts of complaints usually go to Darryn's office, though, and are easily dealt with. I've never had someone complain about me to the school board before. And what for? I've had absolutely no problems with any of my students lately.

He nods. "I'm going to make some calls and see if I can find out more. I really don't like the idea of you being blindsided tonight—I don't like the idea of *me* being blindsided tonight. But I thought I'd let you know first in case you needed to make arrangements."

The bell rings before I can reply, and I turn back to dismiss my class. Several of them are watching us with curious expressions. Darryn doesn't often appear in classrooms without prior warning, and especially not for hushed private conversations.

I need a distraction. "I'll see you tomorrow, everyone. Homework tonight is to punctuate the worksheet I gave you earlier—and anyone who's interested in extra credit this semester can write an essay about the Oxford comma." There's a mixed reaction to that, and I feel as though this might be an assignment that will get more students than usual thinking about extra credit—if only so they can prove to their classmates that their opinion is the "right" one.

Finally, all the students have filed out, most of them with a nod and a farewell to me and Darryn, and he closes the door and follows me to the desk. "Do you have any idea what this could be about?" he asks. "I did a check, but there have been no complaints to the office about you since last year."

I shake my head. "Everything's been good," I confirm. "No disciplinary problems. A few of the students aren't working up to their potential, but I had a quiet chat with two of them and we worked out what the issue was. I even got a call from one's parents to thank me for taking the time to help."

He sighs heavily. "Who knows, then. I guess I'll make those calls and see if anything comes out."

I feel a faint niggle of uncertainty. "You don't think it's because I'm gay, do you?"

Shock crosses his face, then thoughtfulness. "But you've always been gay. It's nothing new, and you've taught here for years. Plus, the school is quite open about the fact that we have several LGBTQ+ staff members. We pride ourselves on our diversity policy."

"Yes, but me being gay has never been so... overt, I suppose. Before, my personal life was something separate from the school. Now that Dom and I are together, it's very much in everyone's face. Mostly through their own efforts," I add, somewhat bitterly, because the constant interest in my relationship can get a bit much sometimes.

"I suppose it's possible." Darryn looks doubtful. "In that case, the board just may want to make you aware of the complaint. They absolutely can't have any problem with you being gay and in a relationship, especially since there's been no negative publicity."

I'm not convinced. I doubt the board would insist on me being there—and refuse to give Darryn more information—if they just wanted to make me aware that someone's complained. This seems a little more serious than that. "We won't know until tonight," I concede, and he grumbles an agreement on his way out the door.

DOM TEXTS me while I wait outside the meeting room at the town hall. The Joyville Public Schools Board meets there every month, and I'm foolishly annoyed that they didn't decide to move their meetings to the high school, as they discussed a couple years ago. It would have been much more convenient for me tonight.

Dom: Have you gone in yet?

Me: Not yet. Meeting just started a few minutes ago. Hopefully won't be long.

I'd gotten some nods and a few curious looks from the board members who weren't already inside when I arrived, but there was no animosity. I really have no idea what this could be about. My union rep, after fretting because she's at a conference in Atlanta and couldn't come with me, gave me a quick list of dos and don'ts over the phone and assured me she'd have my back.

When I called Dom during my free period to tell him I wouldn't be over until later, and why, he went straight into what I call "the director" mode. After firing off a dozen questions, he reminded me that nobody could discriminate against me for being gay and that we'd sue the town into bankruptcy if they tried. That made me laugh, and I assured him it was unlikely to get that far—if that was even the problem at all.

Then he remembered that officially, he's a member of the school board. It seems that the director of JU is a member of every town board, since JU built the town and owns the land it sits on. That was something that happened back at the beginning and never changed, although he's a non-voting member and the director usually only ever attends one meeting a year. He was all prepared to attend tonight's meeting, but I insisted that he not. How unprofessional would it look for me if I call in my influential boyfriend to rescue me? Especially since we still don't know what the problem is.

My phone vibrates again.

Dom: It's probably nothing. Later we'll be laughing at how worried we are now.

Me: Probably. I hope so.

No sooner have I hit Send than the door opens and one of the board members pokes her head out. "Would you join us, please?" she asks, and I get up and follow her in.

The board members and Darryn are seated around a long oval table, and after my guide retakes her seat, there's only one chair left—at the end. I'm definitely the focus of all eyes.

"Thank you for coming this evening," the chairman says smoothly. I've met him a few times at various school events, but we've never really spoken beyond pleasantries.

"You're welcome," I reply. "I have to admit, I'm rather concerned. There was a complaint?" I want to get right to business.

He nods solemnly. "Yes, I'm afraid so. Not about your teaching. It was suggested that you may have used your influence unfairly as regards your, er, partner's daughter."

It takes far longer than it should for the words to sink in. This is about *Cara*?

"I don't understand," I say bluntly, and two of the board members exchange significant glances. I know those two—they're the ones who objected vociferously to some of the new books we included on the recommended reading lists, claiming they were inappropriate. Sticks in the mud, both of them.

Wait a second—

"Cara Hurst is Dominic Hurst's daughter, correct?" the chairman asks, and I drag my attention back to him.

"Yes. Until recently, that wasn't widely known, as she didn't wish to receive any special treatment."

The woman who showed me in smiles at the tabletop. I don't know her, but I get the feeling she could be an ally.

"Commendable," the chairman comments. "You were aware, however."

"Of course. I think it's widely known that Dom-inic and I are in a relationship, and as you say, she *is* his daughter." I hope they don't notice the little stumble over his name. I decided at the last second that the extra two syllables would add weight to his influence here, ridiculous as it sounds. "However, she's not in any of my classes. I rarely see her during school hours, if ever." I hesitate. "I might be able to help clear this up faster if you could tell me specifically what the complaint was about." Does one of Cara's classmates think she didn't deserve one of her grades? I don't have anything to do with grading Cara. This seems like a petty waste of time.

"The complaint was that you are in a position to show favoritism to Miss Hurst and have done so in the past."

"If I may interrupt," Darryn says, sitting forward, "Oliver and I discussed this situation when he began seeing Dominic Hurst. Cara is in none of Oliver's classes, so that was not something we felt the need to consider, but even if she were, we have had teachers who were parents of students in the past. It's not always possible for them to be in different classes, so there is a protocol in place to ensure there is no favoritism in grading. I'm not sure what the problem is here. This complaint seems empty to me."

Several of the board members are nodding, which is a huge relief. The chairman seems thoughtful.

And then one of the sticks opens his mouth. "But Mr. Jeffries is the head of the English department and could use his influence there in Miss Hurst's favor."

I see red.

Fortunately, I'm not the only one, and Darryn's quicker to open his mouth than I am. "That's quite an offensive comment, to Oliver, to the teachers who work with him, and to me. I can assure you that no teacher at my school would allow a personal connection to cause them to pressure a colleague, nor would they allow themselves to be so pressured. Unless you have specific evidence of an assignment being misgraded that you would like to present, this seems rather petty. We live in a relatively small community here, and our teachers are people too. Of course they have connections outside the school. We trust that they put those aside when it comes time to assess their students, and for the most part, that has been the case. In all the years Oliver has been teaching at Joyville High, there has never been a complaint of him showing favoritism."

The stick smirks, an ugly little expression that makes me want to smack him. "And yet, that's exactly what this is. I've been advised that in October of last year, Mr. Jeffries intervened on Miss Hurst's behalf in a disciplinary matter, and as a result, one of the teachers in his department was reprimanded."

It hits me in a rush. The sticks were close friends of Howard Hamilton, who was a member of the board until he died a few years ago. Who was Edith Hamilton's husband.

I look at Darryn, who's looking back at me, then turns to address the stick.

"If you had advised me of your information before this meeting," he says calmly, "I could have told you the details of that particular event and we could have saved Oliver the need to attend. Oliver did not, in fact, intervene in a disciplinary matter. Miss Hurst received a detention from Mrs. Hamilton"—there's a tiny rustle as the rest of the board suddenly realizes exactly what's going on—"and she served that detention. I believe she also apologized to Mrs. Hamilton and was disciplined further by her father. Is that correct, Oliver?"

I nod. "So I was told at the time. It happened well before my relationship with Dominic began, so I couldn't say firsthand."

"What was the reprimand for, then?" the chairman asks, cutting off the stick before he can say more.

"I issued the reprimand," Darryn declares, "when it was brought to my attention that Mrs. Hamilton said something truly offensive to Mr. Hurst during their meeting."

"And there you have it," the stick announces triumphantly. "On the word of Dominic Hurst, a teacher was reprimanded."

There are many puzzled expressions around the table. "Are you saying that you think Mr. Hurst was lying?" one of the other board members asks. "And if so, why would he do that?"

"Before you answer," Darryn says, and there's fire in

his eyes now. He's usually the most even-tempered of people, but this has gone too far. "You should know that I had a private meeting with Mrs. Hamilton at the time, and she did not dispute that she made the comment. She also had the right—as do all our staff—to appeal the reprimand officially, and she chose not to do so. Her only complaint to me then was that Cara Hurst was a disruptive influence in her class. Miss Hurst was moved from her class that same day."

"Moved by Mr. Jeffries." The stick is still smirking.

Darryn raises a brow. "After discussion with me and with Cara, yes. It was agreed that moving Cara would be beneficial for the class and for her. Mrs. Hamilton did not disagree."

"You see?" The stick—damn, I wish I remembered his name—sweeps his gaze around the table. "Mr. Jeffries was making special allowances for Miss Hurst."

"I don't know about that," the woman who showed me in says slowly. "It doesn't seem like an allowance. Students have been moved between classes before due to personality clashes with classmates and teachers."

"Ah," the stick holds up a finger as though he's some kind of supervillain, "but Miss Hurst's grades have noticeably improved since the move."

"How do you know that?" I ask sharply, and the room falls silent.

"Yes," Darryn chimes in. "Student grades are confidential."

The stick turns red. "I made a request to the school office," he blusters. "The board is within its rights to do so."

"Usually those requests are channeled through me," Darryn says.

"And me," the chairman adds, giving the stick a dark look.

"Who handled your request? I'll ensure they're reminded about the proper process." Darryn knows, of course, that no such request was ever made. Edith pulled Cara's grades, which isn't against the rules, but it's definitely not ethical. There's no reason for her to be logging into the files of students she doesn't teach, and she definitely shouldn't be sharing information from them with anyone, member of the board or not.

The other stick—Stick Two?—speaks up then. "We're digressing. The relevant point is that Mr. Jeffries used his influence to move Miss Hurst to another class and her grades improved. Surely that shows that things are not aboveboard."

Marcus Finch, who's the head librarian at the town library, speaks up. "Actually, it makes sense to me that Miss Hurst's grades would improve after she left a class that wasn't right for her. That often happens, correct?"

Darryn nods. "Correct. If students are finding the classroom uncomfortable, it can affect their work. A change in situation almost always results in a difference."

Marcus looks around the table. "This seems more likely than two of our very reputable teachers conspiring to falsify grades. Are Miss Hurst's grades in this particular class inconsistent with those in her other classes?"

"I haven't reviewed her file," Darryn says, "since I wasn't told it would be necessary, but as far as I'm aware, the only class she ever had any problems with, in regard to learning or behavior, was Mrs. Hamilton's."

"And we all know this isn't the first time a student has had problems with Edith Hamilton," mutters my ally, the woman who invited me in. I should really find out her name.

"How dare you impugn Mrs. Hamilton?" gasps Stick One.

"Mrs. Hamilton has been a teacher at Joyville High since it opened," Stick Two adds. "She has nurtured the minds of countless students and is deserving of our utmost respect!"

"We're getting off topic," the chairman says hastily. "It seems that there's no specific issue here. Unless proof can be provided of favoritism, which I don't believe it can, there's nothing to discuss."

"Of course proof can be provided," Stick One scoffs. "We merely need to have Miss Hurst's assessments independently reviewed."

Another silence falls around the table.

"I'd like to ensure I have this clear," Darryn says carefully. "You are accusing Oliver Jeffries, as head of the English department, of coercing or otherwise influencing one of the teachers reporting to him to change Cara Hurst's grades? And you are accusing one of my other teachers of grading a student beyond what she has earned?"

Stick One nods. "I am."

"These are very serious accusations," the chairman says. "Be very sure you're making them on firm grounds."

"We have no doubt they will prove to be correct," Stick Two declares.

"Well, I do. I have many doubts," Marcus counters. "Perhaps you can tell us why you're so sure? Because if I remember correctly, an independent review of a student's grades can only be undertaken if there are solid grounds to do so and after the student and their family has been advised. So far, I haven't been told anything that would suffice as 'solid grounds,' and if we proceed anyway and it turns out you're wrong, not only will you have wrongly accused two upstanding teachers, you'll also have made an enemy of Dominic Hurst."

"There. See?" Stick Two points. "That is exactly the problem. Are we afraid to take disciplinary action against students for fear of who their parents are? Dominic Hurst's position at Joy Universe should have no influence on the decision we make here tonight."

A headache stabs behind my right eye.

"You're right," my ally agrees, "Dominic Hurst's position shouldn't have any influence on our decision. But it seems to me that Cara Hurst is being singled out here because of her father's position—or perhaps because he's dating Mr. Jeffries? You've yet to provide evidence that anything untoward has occurred. I'm also still uncertain where the complaint originated from." She looks to the chairman, who turns resignedly to the sticks.

Stick One says stiffly, "It was anonymous."

A sigh/groan goes around the table. It's obvious to everyone that Edith Hamilton has gone on the warpath —for one thing, the only people who knew about that reprimand were her, me, and Darryn, and I doubt Darryn said anything to the sticks about it. I just don't understand what set Edith off—and what her end game is.

"I'd like to understand," I begin, and all eyes come to me, "what outcome you'd like to see. I have not treated Cara Hurst differently from any other student. There is no evidence that I have. You could have Cara's work independently assessed and that would prove to be the case, but an anonymous complaint that I favor her with no accompanying evidence doesn't seem to be sufficient grounds to do so." I flick a glance at Darryn, who nods slightly.

"Of course you'd say that," Stick Two says acidly, and I wonder why these two have gone all supervillain. Is it because I campaigned so hard for those new reading lists? Do they really hate me because I wanted to add some fantasy novels written by women within the last thirty years? Because I campaigned for some young adult novels that feature—gasp—kissing and sexual references?

"Okay," the chairman intervenes. "Let's not get nasty. We'll vote if we have to, but I think most of us agree that there's not enough here to warrant an assessment of Miss Hurst's work. Yes?" He looks around the table and is met with nods from all but the sticks and one other person. "So—"

"If I may," the third person who didn't nod, an older woman in a twinset, interrupts. "Perhaps we could ask Mr. Singh to undertake a quiet review of Miss Hurst's file and speak with her teachers. If it seems that there is anything irregular, we can revisit the possibility of an independent assessment next month."

The chairman glances around again. "That seems reasonable." When nobody objects, he adds, "Darryn, please see to it."

Darryn nods. "Of course." He makes a note, although I honestly don't think this is something he'll forget.

"With that being the case, let's defer any further discussion of this complaint until next month."

Stick Two's eyebrows would have risen to his hairline if he still had any hair. "Don't you think it's inadvisable to allow Mr. Jeffries to continue in his current position given these allegations?"

The room actually spins around me as those words hit with the force of a sledgehammer. He wants me *fired*?

"That's an extreme reaction," Marcus says. "There's no evidence that Oliver has done anything wrong. In fact, the only *allegation* he's done anything wrong is an 'anonymous' one and extremely vague. If it were up to me, the complaint would already have been dismissed and Oliver wouldn't even have been called in here."

Stick Two plants his hands on the table, and once again the chairman speaks before anyone can say anything damning. Honestly, I had no idea board meetings were so volatile. I'd be amused if it wasn't my future hanging in the balance.

"Until we can show that there's just cause for Mr. Jeffries to be disciplined in any way, we cannot ethically take action. I move that all discussion of this complaint be deferred until next month."

"I second," Marcus announces, and then they vote. I'm heartened to see that only the sticks vote nay.

The chairman smiles at me. "Thank you for coming tonight. I'll ask that you not speak of this to anyone while the situation is under investigation." There's a warning glint in his eyes, and although the words are general, we all know he's telling me I can't discuss what happened here with Dom.

I stiffen my spine. "People are aware that a complaint was made against me and that's why I had to attend tonight. But I'll keep the details of the complaint to myself—except for my union rep, of course." I don't wait for a response, getting up and walking out without saying anything else. What would I have said?

On my way to the car, I send Darryn a text thanking him for standing up for me. He probably won't see it until the meeting's done, but that's okay. I don't really want to talk anyway. It's enough that I have to weasel out of giving Dom any details *and* wait a month to have this whole debacle settled.

In the car, I just sit for a minute, letting my brain catch up. There's no doubt in my head that Edith put her husband's friends up to this. They're the reason she hasn't been forced to retire before now; they're the reason she's gotten by with so few warnings, despite the number of complaints about her. It fits the pattern that they would step in to forcibly ram through a complaint with no substance if she was the one who made it.

But why did she make it?

Edith and I have had our problems—we'll never be friends—but I always thought she respected me as a teacher, at least. The thing with Cara was months ago—why suddenly resurrect it now? Does she truly, honestly think I pressured Jaiden to falsify Cara's grades?

None of it makes sense.

Sighing, I start the car and head to Dom's place. Even if I can't tell him anything, I'd rather be there with him than home alone.

He meets me at the door with a hug, and I melt into his arms. It feels so good to be held.

"What happened?" he asks when I finally step back, and I shake my head.

"They decided to investigate further, so it's been deferred until next month. I can't share the details."

His eyes narrow. "They called you in without even having investigated if the complaint was valid?"

"Dom, I really can't talk about it."

He tips his head to the side and studies me, and I know he sees how exhausted I feel. It's mental exhaustion, since it's really not that late.

"Come and eat. I kept some dinner for you."

"That sounds wonderful," I moan and follow him to the kitchen. He busies himself getting a serving dish out of the oven and ladling out what smells like some kind of stew. I sit at the table and try not to drool. I hadn't realized how hungry I was until this moment—maybe some food will help me feel better.

Dom sets the bowl and a spoon in front of me, and I dig in while he gets me water and a glass.

"You're amazing," I mutter between spoonfuls, and he just smiles.

Finally I'm done, and I sit back with a sigh of contentment.

"More?" he asks, and it's tempting, but I shake my head.

"No, thank you. I might steal a cookie later, though." Tonight feels like a gratuitous cookie night.

"They're all yours," he promises, then reaches out and captures my hand. "Oliver… you know I'm on the school board, right?"

Damn, I thought he'd let that go. "We've talked about this," I say quietly, sliding my hand out of his grasp. "I don't need you fighting my battles."

He shakes his head. "No, what I mean is, as a board member, even a non-voting one, I have access to the minutes of board meetings."

I freeze.

Crap.

I did *not* think of that.

I meet his gaze. "Please don't."

He sits back, shocked. "You don't want me to…? I just meant that since I had access to the information anyway, you could discuss it with me, but you actually don't want me to know?" Hurt is clear in his tone, and I wish this awful, horrible day would just *end*, already.

"I…" What do I say? Of course I want to discuss it with him. But he's going to be livid, especially when he hears that Cara is involved. I honestly don't think there's any chance of her being affected by this—if I did, I'd be telling him everything and letting him loose to annihilate the sticks. If I *don't* tell him, though, will he go and read the minutes and find out anyway? Which option is worse?

Can I fudge this? Tell him someone is disputing a student's grade and just not give more information? But he'll wonder why I couldn't tell him that much to begin with.

This sucks. This whole day is just garbage.

"I… I want you to know, but I want to be able to tell you. After it's all over. So I'm going to ask you to please not look at the meeting minutes." As soon as the words are out, I want to snatch them back. I know they'll hurt him. I know it's all pointless anyway—he'll have to find out eventually. But I'm feeling worn down and bruised by what happened tonight, by the fact that I have to wait another month to see what the outcome will be, and I know if Dom finds out, he's going to be pissed. He's going to be an angry father and an angry boyfriend, and he's going to want to charge in and demand a resolution *now*. It's going to look like I need my boyfriend to fight my battles. People will wonder if I'm using his influence as the director to hide the possibility that it's true. And I just don't have the energy right now to talk Dom into letting things play out.

So I don't apologize and take it back.

The words sit between us like lead weights. I can't meet his gaze.

Finally, Dom says, "If that's what you want. I just want you to be okay."

Could anything make me feel worse than hearing those words?

I force myself to look him in the eye. "Thank you."

He sends me off to have a long, hot shower while he cleans up the kitchen, and then we settle on the couch to watch mindless TV. There's a stack of assignments I should be grading, but it's just not going to happen tonight. I just stare at the TV, not really sure what we're watching and wishing that there wasn't this sudden awkwardness between me and Dom. Is this our first fight? It can't be—neither of us yelled. But it feels like we're fighting.

My phone chimes, and I almost leap from the couch. I've never been so relieved to get a text before, and I'm not even sure why—we were just sitting. I aim a plastic smile at Dom and go dig my phone from my laptop bag.

The text is from Darryn.

You've done nothing wrong. This whole thing is ridiculous. Logged on to the server as soon as I got home and had a look at C's file—grades are consistent across all classes. Will talk with her teachers tomorrow, but I'm certain you have nothing to worry about. Will try to get the board to meet again about this early so you can put it behind you.

I press my hand to my stomach, where the knot

that's been tormenting me for hours has suddenly dissolved. I hadn't realized, but on some level I must have been worried that Cara's grades weren't within the same range in all her classes. That's dumb, because I actually know for a fact that she gets good grades, since I'm usually here when her dad asks her about them, and I definitely know I didn't pressure Jaiden into giving her better grades than she deserves, but still there was that fear.

I text Darryn back.

Thanks for checking tonight. Please don't do anything that's going to cause trouble for you on the board—it can wait until next month.

I hesitate, then add, *Dom asked me about the meeting, and when I said I couldn't talk about it, he reminded me that technically he's a board member. I asked him not to read the minutes.*

I'm not sure why I've said that. Dom's not going to read the minutes, so it's all fine. There's nothing for Darryn to need to know.

The dots are dancing, though, which means Darryn's already texting back.

It's probably best that way—gives us a chance to resolve this before he blows his stack. If you want to tell him, though, you should. The board is aware that he has access to the minutes.

I think about it. I could turn around, go back to the couch, curl up against Dom, and unload this hell on his strong shoulders. I'd be able to share my burdens with my partner—isn't that one of the benefits of being in a relationship?

But nothing would have changed. He'll still be angry. He won't be okay with letting me and Darryn fix this. And I don't want to have to deal with that right now.

Not tonight. Maybe in a few days. Thanks again. See you tomorrow.

I get a thumbs-up in acknowledgment, then put the phone down and go back to the couch.

Where I sit with six whole inches between me and Dom.

I hate this day.

THIRTEEN

Dom

_____

I've been distracted all morning. No, I take that back —I've been distracted since Oliver called me yesterday to tell me that he had to attend the school board meeting because someone made a complaint about him. It seemed surreal to me—still does. Who'd complain about him? I mean, I might be biased, but really, what's there to complain about? He's a dedicated and enthusiastic teacher. His students mostly love him —_and_ they do well in state testing. He willingly gives of his time to the school for extracurricular activities. Seriously, why would anyone make a complaint to the board?

Unless it's about me. I don't like to think that someone would be that small-minded or petty, but it happens. People can really suck. And sometimes they get it in their heads that they have the right to dictate things like who their kid's teacher should be allowed to date.

So, yeah, I was distracted all yesterday afternoon. Then I was on tenterhooks waiting for Oliver to get home and tell me what happened. Which ended up with me still being on tenterhooks but also feeling kind of sick. How bad is it that he doesn't want me to know? Could he lose his job over this? It's probably about me, right? Why else would he not want me to know?

I didn't sleep well last night.

I hate that he's so stressed by this, even though he's trying to pretend he isn't. When he decided to go home instead of staying over, even though he was clearly exhausted and had to drag himself out the door, I knew it was even worse than I'd been imagining. So I was up half the night trying to decide what my options would be—which is hard when I don't even know what the problem is.

As a result of all the stress and sleeplessness, this morning has not been productive. Layla's guessed that something's going on and has asked me a few times if everything's okay. I'm not prepared to share Oliver's problems with her when he doesn't even want to share them with me, so all I can do is smile and say, "Sure, it's fine," and try to drag my brain back into gear.

Then my email pinged.

It does that a lot, but it's still automatic for me to glance at it and make sure it's not urgent—even though I know most people will call or text for anything time sensitive.

So I glanced. I wasn't expecting anything that needed my immediate attention. And I was right.

But now I can't drag my gaze away from the screen. I can't click back over to the finance report I was reading. All I can do is stare at the innocent email that feels like a ticking time bomb.

From: Joyville Public Schools Board
Subject: Minutes of Monthly Meeting

The body of the email is the same generic message as every month—please find attached blah blah blah. It's the attached document that's screaming at me.

In that attachment are the answers to my questions. The answer to why Oliver was called in. To who complained about him, and why. Knowledge is power, and with that knowledge, I could help. I could take this burden from him and possibly do something to fix the situation.

But I promised him I wouldn't look.

Is this like when you teach your kid to ride a bike and they make you promise not to let go, but as soon as you're sure they're steady, you do?

"Hey, got a second?"

I make a high-pitched noise and jerk back from my desk. "Nothing!"

Oh, fuck.

As the adrenaline drains away, I huff a laugh and press my fingertips to my eyes for a second. "Come in," I tell Luke, who's looking at me like I've got a few screws loose.

"Everything okay?" he asks, closing the door behind him and coming to take a seat.

I paste on a fake smile. "Sure, it's fine," I say, then hesitate. "Hey, you're in a committed relationship."

He blinks. "Yes," he replies cautiously.

I forge on, because I've already made an idiot of myself and he's the closest friend I've got here in Joyville, aside from Cara and Oliver, neither of whom I can discuss this with.

"You know how a relationship is supposed to be based on trust and honesty?"

"I think I'm out of my depth," he mutters, but I ignore him.

"Let's say you made a promise to Grant. I'm not talking about the big ones like fidelity—this is a little promise. Like… he's bought your birthday present and hidden it in the house, and you promised not to go searching for it." That is not a good analogy.

Luke looks confused but nods. "Okay."

"But then you realize that every time the subject of your birthday comes up, Grant gets more and more stressed. It's genuinely affecting him, and you want to help, but he won't tell you what's wrong."

"Oh… kay. He's… stressed about my birthday?"

I ignore the interruption. "And you're pretty sure that if you find your birthday present, you'll know why he's upset, and maybe you'll be able to help and fix things so he's not stressed." Yep, it's a terrible analogy. Luke must think so too, because he's staring blankly at me.

"But didn't I promise not to look for my birthday present?" he asks.

"Yes!" I point at him. "Yes. But if it's causing problems for him, isn't there a relationship loophole that lets you break that promise? So you can help him?" My gaze sneaks sideways to the enormous monitor, where "the email" is still prominently displayed.

Luke sighs. "I feel like you want me to say yes, but Dom, unless Grant's safety was at risk, I really wouldn't break a promise like that. We had problems last year because our—*my*—communication wasn't as great as it should have been, and we've made a commitment to discussing problems openly. If Grant really didn't want to share something and I was worried about how it was affecting him, I'd tell him." He shrugs. "I can't say what would happen or how it would turn out, because we haven't been in that situation."

I'm not really surprised. I know I wouldn't like it if Oliver broke a promise like that to me. I stare at the screen, my fingers twitching to open that attachment. I guess the question is, how willing am I to deal with the fallout?

"Wanna tell me about it?" Luke asks quietly. "Is Oliver okay?"

Now it's my turn to sigh. "Between us?" He nods. "He got called before the school board last night, supposedly about a complaint. He was stressed and really down when he got home, said things had been deferred until next month pending further investigation, and told me he couldn't talk about it."

"That sucks. Who would complain about him, anyway? The kids all love him. Mila says he's the second-most popular teacher at the school, after the art teacher who lets them throw water balloons full of paint at the walls."

"Say what?" I'm momentarily distracted. Cara never mentioned throwing paint, but then again, I don't think she's taking any art classes this year. Still, none of my teachers ever let me throw paint at walls.

"Focus," he chides. "So he can't tell you because he's been told not to discuss it?"

I nod. "Yes. But the thing is, I'm technically a school board member. I can't vote, but I'm permitted to attend all the meetings, and they send me the minutes." My gaze darts quickly to the screen, and when I look back at Luke, I can tell he didn't miss the gesture.

"They're right there in front of you, aren't they?"

I nod.

"Have you read them yet?"

I shake my head.

"But you want to."

Another nod.

"Fuck, Dom."

Yeah.

"I can't tell you what to do, but you need to think about this carefully. What if you look at them and there's nothing you can do? You'll have to deal with knowing you broke your promise for nothing. And could you keep that secret from Oliver?"

I grimace. "I hadn't thought of that." Could I break my promise and then never tell Oliver about it?

Probably not. It might be okay at first, but over time, it would eat at me. Hell, I already feel guilty just for thinking about it.

On the other hand... if I can do something to help—

"And even if you can help," Luke goes on, as though he can read my mind, "Oliver might not want you to. He's not an idiot. He has a good idea of what your capabilities are, and if he wanted you to step in, he wouldn't have asked you not to read the minutes. So you'll have broken your promise and will be potentially stepping on his toes. I don't think he'll thank you for it."

I narrow my eyes at him. "You're not helping."

He huffs a laugh. "If the help you want is permission to break a promise to your boyfriend, that's something you have to do for yourself."

Groaning, I slump back in my chair. "Yeah. I'll talk to him tonight." Reaching over, I grab the mouse and move the cursed email to the folder that has all the other school board stuff. "Okay, now that we're done with my personal drama, was there something you needed?"

He levels me with a look. "You sure you're okay?"

I start to fake smile, then stop. Friends, right? "Not really, but I will be. I'm just worried about Oliver. Guess we'll just have to wait until next month."

Luke studies me for a few more seconds, then says, "If there's anything you guys need, we're here. You know Dimi would love to organize a protest or whatever."

We laugh, because we can both imagine Dimi with a megaphone rallying the masses, and I say, "Hopefully it won't come to that, but maybe we should keep it in mind just for kicks. Now… what's up?"

As he launches into a description of the latest problem the audit team's discovered, I push all thoughts of the meeting minutes to the back of my mind. I need to talk to Oliver again.

OLIVER TEXTS me right after school lets out to say he doesn't think he'll come over tonight. As my stomach sinks in typical lead-brick fashion, I try to think how I can fix this. He's stressed, and I probably didn't help things last night by pushing him to talk to me.

Which means I need to let go of this and let him deal with it his way. I start to call, but then decide to text back. Maybe he doesn't feel like talking right now. A text will give him more processing time than a call would, anyway.

Dom: If that's what you want. Just want you to know that I missed you last night, and I'm sorry I pressured you to tell me what happened at the meeting. If you change your mind, no matter what time, I'll be glad to see you.

There. That's supportive, right? Unless…

Dom: Or if you'd rather stay home but want some company, I could come round after dinner?

Cara's home tonight, and I won't ditch her completely—only a few months until graduation—but she'll have homework and whatever garbage reality show she's watching at the moment and marathon texting with her friends to keep her busy after we eat. She won't care if I'm out for a few hours.

I make myself put my phone down instead of staring at the screen and waiting for him to reply. I texted instead of calling so he could have processing time, so now I have to allow him that time.

And I have to accept that the ball is in his court on this. It's *his* work issue. If he doesn't want to talk about it, doesn't want me to get involved in any way, that's his call. I can't take over.

My phone chimes, and I snatch it up so fast, I fumble and drop it.

Oliver: Let me see how this grading goes. If I get enough done, I'll come over.

The grin that stretches my mouth is so wide, it almost hurts. I hated how things were last night. Hated the distance between us on the couch, and worse, the emotional distance. Hated that he went home instead of staying. Hated that when he left, things were strained between us. All I want is to make things better for him, and if that means being supportive in the background, I can do that.

I can.

Oliver turns up at the condo right before dinner, looking pale and tired but otherwise okay. He smiles at Cara and asks what she's cooking, managing to do so in a way that distracts from the fact that he hasn't kissed me, has barely looked in my direction.

So when Cara turns back to the stove, I close the small distance between me and Oliver, ignoring the trepidation in his eyes, and bend my head to bury my face in his neck. "Sorry," I mutter, keeping my voice down so Cara doesn't hear. "I shouldn't have pushed. I just… I'm sorry."

He expels this huge breath, and his arms come around me. "Me too," he whispers. "Just… please let me handle this."

I nod against his neck. "Whatever you want. Missed you so much." It's stupid, because we don't spend every night together anyway, but last night was different. The absence was more than physical.

He squeezes, but before he can say anything, Cara turns around and says, "Aww… look, as cute as you both are, watching my dad and his boyfriend cuddle is not on my list of fun stuff to do."

Oliver snorts and pulls back. "I'd be worried if it was," he teases, and I'm pretty sure she can't see that his eyes are a little wet.

We set the table while my beloved daughter regales us with the latest lunchtime drama—I'm so glad my days of eating in school cafeterias are behind me—and then we sit down to eat. Cara's feeling chatty and social tonight, so Oliver and I barely get a word in edgewise through dinner and cleanup. I'm not complaining—I love seeing my daughter so animated and happy—but at the same time, I'm glad when she takes herself off to her room.

"I need to tell you," Oliver begins as I turn on the TV and sink onto the couch. He's hovering, wringing his hands a little. "It's good. I mean, it should be good. Darryn was able to get some information that should settle this. He's waiting to talk to one more person, but he's already contacted the chairman of the board and asked for a special meeting to resolve everything so it won't have to wait until next month."

"That's great." I'm surprised, frankly. When he said they wanted to investigate further, I envisioned it being something complex. If the info they needed could be so easily found, it begs the question of why it wasn't properly investigated before they dragged him to the meeting and put him through this. "Do you think they'll agree to a special meeting?"

He shrugs and seems to relax a little, his muscles unknotting as he perches beside me. "I don't know. If they don't, it won't kill me to wait. It would be nice to have this over with, though."

I lean over and kiss him. "I know."

Settling properly onto the couch, he slumps against me. "I want to be able to talk to you about this."

"And you will," I promise. "When you're ready. I'm so sorry about last night. I don't want—"

"I know. I might have overreacted a bit. You weren't pushy, but I was tired and a bit shaken from the meeting. Let's just forget about it."

I kiss him again, and we do. We let it go and bicker about what to watch and spend the evening in front of the TV like an old married couple before we go to bed together. It's so much better than last night.

We murmur softly to each other in the dark, stupid things, reminders about the opening night of the next JVTC show and thoughts about whether he's due a haircut or if he can wait another week. Just ordinary things that pop into our heads as our brains begin to unwind for sleep.

I'm nearly under when I feel him shift up on his elbow beside me, and I want to open my eyes and look at him, but my lids are too heavy. I can hear him, though, when he whispers, "I won't let them do this to us."

He settles back to the mattress and rolls over, so he doesn't see my eyes open as adrenaline floods my system.

FOURTEEN

Oliver

I t's not until Monday that Darryn asks me to meet with him in his office during my lunch break. When I spoke to him last Thursday, he was trying to get the board to agree that this complaint needed to be resolved sooner rather than later, but I don't know what happened. Since I haven't been called to an emergency board meeting, I'm guessing they said no.

Which makes this impromptu meeting a little daunting.

I knock on his door and open it at his call. He's already coming around his desk as I walk in, and he claps me on the shoulder and closes the door behind me.

"Thanks for coming, Oliver. I know you have a busy day." The words are normal, and even the actions are, but for some reason, he can't meet my gaze.

I feel a little sick. Is this bad? How can it be bad? I've done nothing wrong.

He gestures me to a chair, and I take it as he goes back around the desk to sit in his. "Okay, well, the good news is, while the board wouldn't agree to a special meeting, they did agree to review the notes I put together about Cara's assessments, including her grades and some letters and comments from her teachers. They did that over the weekend and contacted me this morning to advise that everything looks fine and they don't believe there is evidence of special preference."

The breath bursts out of me, and I slump in relief. "That's great. That's… wow, it feels so good to have that cleared up." I smile at him, and it takes me a second to notice he's not smiling back. In fact, he's swallowing hard and looks a bit ill. "Darryn? That's great news, right?" Belatedly, I remember him starting with "the good news is." Crap. Does that mean there's bad news? How can that be?

I straighten. "Whatever it is, just tell me."

He sucks in a deep breath. "Off the record, I want you to know I protested this. I'm going to continue protesting this. And as your friend, I advise you to get a lawyer."

That doesn't make me feel better. I force the words through my suddenly dry throat. "Tell me."

"This incident has shown the board that there is potential for misunderstandings where a member of the faculty has supervisory or other influence over teachers who assess students with a connection to that member of faculty." He's reading directly off a piece of paper, his voice a monotone, and I'm sure it's meant to convey that this is not something he wants a part of, but it's just making it harder for me to follow what he's saying. "Given that potential, no faculty member with such a connection should hold a position that would give them such influence."

I run the words through my head again. "They've

decided that faculty who have a personal relationship with a student can't be... what? Principal? VP? A department head?" My chest feels tight, and for a brief, horrifying second, I wonder if I'm having a heart attack.

Panic attack, more like, a sensible inner voice says. *Take a deep breath.*

Yeah, easier to think than do.

Darryn nods curtly. "There are a few other job titles on their list, mostly in admin, but yes."

"That's ridiculous! And just as insulting as the initial bullshit complaint!" The curse seems to surprise us both —I'm normally more careful about word choice, especially on school grounds, but if ever the word bullshit was called for, it's now. I say it again for emphasis. "This is bullshit, Darryn."

"I know," he says. "I'm putting together a formal protest from me personally and on behalf of the school. I imagine several other of the staff will also do so once the change is communicated. Some of them have had kids here in the past—their own, or relatives of some kind—and some will in the future. You know we're always very careful about the procedure when teachers' kids are at the school, but this is crossing lines. I truly don't believe it will stand, but until it's officially revoked, we have to abide by it."

I can't think. I just can't...

"So I've been demoted?" It's barely a whisper. I love being the head of the English department. I love the changes I've implemented and the ones I've been planning. This is *bullshit*.

Darryn can't even bring himself to say it. He just jerks his head in a nod.

I swallow hard.

Think.

"Okay, uh... I don't know if you can tell me this or if I need to call the union rep, but what are my options? To protest, I mean." I should know this. I'm sure I do. I've been teaching for a long time, at many schools. But for whatever reason, the correct procedure just won't come to mind.

"Call the union rep," he says immediately. "I probably shouldn't be saying this, but my take is that there were one or two board members who pushed for this, and the others gave in because they were sick of discussing it. I'm almost positive it's not legal, and even if it is, I don't think the board will be willing to fight that hard about it. If you push, if I push, they'll reverse this stupid decision."

"Push, how? Sue, you mean?" I may not be thinking that clearly, but I do know that suing an employer is only a good idea if you don't want to keep working there. Win or lose, it's not easy to work at a company or organization you've just taken through a legal battle.

He shakes his head. "I doubt it will get that far, but making legal noises might help."

I press my hands to my face. "This is a disaster," I mutter, then lower them and look at him. "And until then? I'm just supposed to give up my department role? Who's going to take it over?" Oh my god, the gossip this is going to cause amongst the students. I don't think I can handle this.

Darryn pinches the bridge of his nose, and I'm reminded that this is going to cause chaos for him too. Not as much as me, but still...

"I don't know," he admits. "I feel like an ass even saying this, but do you have any recommendations?"

It's a punch to the gut. Even if it's just an interim appointment, that person—the person he wants me to recommend—would be taking *my* job.

"I'm sorry. I shouldn't have asked. I'm so sorry."

"No," I mutter. "Uh. Let me… let me think about it." Because I want the right person to be looking after things until I can take the job back.

If I can.

Oh my god.

I wish I were anywhere other than here right now.

I lurch to my feet. "Darryn, I'm sorry. I have to go. I have to…" Crap, I have afternoon classes.

Am I really in the right frame of mind to teach them?

If I was sick, I'd go home. Or if there was an emergency. What's this, if not stricken by an unspeakable crisis?

I open my mouth to ask him to find someone to cover my classes for the rest of the day, but the words won't come. I can't walk away from my students like that. More, I *won't* give Stick One and Stick Two and the idiots on the board who let themselves be bullied into doing this the satisfaction of saying I couldn't cope.

It might be stupid pride, but right now, it feels like the only thing I have. I'm not letting it go.

"I need to make some calls before lunch ends," I finally say. "I'll have a recommendation for you by the end of the day." I honestly have no idea who it will be, because right now, I'm struggling to even remember who's in my department, but I *will* pull myself together. I just need a few minutes to myself.

Darryn seems to get it, because he nods and says something about compiling his protest, and then I'm out of his office. I smile at Maria. I nod as I pass one of the science teachers in the hall. In fact, I'm pretty sure I do a good job of being normal.

Until I get to my office. Which is actually no longer my office. Only department heads have offices; the rest of the faculty just have their classrooms.

That's fine. I don't have many personal items here—it's mostly school stuff. I can just move back to my class-room for the time being.

My hands start shaking slightly, and I automatically reach for my phone. I really want to call Dom. He'll know what to do. Hell, he probably already knows whether this is legal or not.

But if I call him now, he'll blow off work for the rest of the day to come and sort this out, and I've already decided I'm staying until school finishes. Plus, there's a good chance I'm going to get emotional when I tell him, and I'm not ready for that right now. I can talk to him tonight.

It's all going to be fine.

I grab the landline and call the union rep. I have to leave a message, and I ask her to call me back on my cell. Then, on a whim, I call Sascha Weston. She would know better than anyone in town who's who on the school board, and I'm probably going to need information. The manager of her boutique says she's meeting with a supplier, and I leave a message for her to call me. Idly, I wonder why Sascha's not on the school board. I seem to remember she was at one stage—maybe she resigned when her kids were all done with the school?

Sighing, I sit back in my chair and wonder what the best next step is. Lunch will be over soon and—

"I'm surprised you haven't started packing."

I jerk and look toward the doorway. Edith stands there, her eyes narrowed.

"Edith, I… What did you say?" Did she just…?

She sniffs. "I heard you've been demoted. You should have been fired."

Oh my god. Where did this come from? *Why?*

"Why should I have been fired?" I manage to ask calmly. "I've done nothing wrong."

"You're dating a parent of a student at this school," she snaps. "How can you say that's not wrong?"

"Not a student I teach," I point out slowly. "And even if it was a student I teach, there are procedures to allow for that."

"It's unacceptable," she insists. "Completely unethical."

I'm not sure what code of ethics she's referring to, but I can tell it's not an argument I'll win. She's chosen this hill to die on, for whatever reason, and the fact that I've done nothing to breach school policy wasn't enough for her—she had to go whining to the board so they'd make one up that I was in breach of.

I've got better and more important things to do than argue with someone who's out to make trouble.

"I just want to know," I begin, "why this is suddenly a problem for you now. I've been dating Dom for months."

She sticks her nose in the air. "I wasn't aware until recently. Unlike many here, I don't insist on knowing all the details of my colleagues' personal lives."

That's a nice way of saying she doesn't give a shit about us. It's not like this is something only a few people knew—it's very public and has been discussed a lot.

Regardless, she's not worth any more of my time.

"Was there something you wanted, Edith?"

She seems taken aback and stammers for a moment. "I-I came to tell you that you should be ashamed, and that demoting you was the right decision."

Hold on.

I narrow my eyes. "Who told you I was being demoted?" I know, of course. It's too soon for Darryn to have made an announcement to the staff—and he won't use the word "demoted" when he does. The sticks probably called her as soon as the board made the decision.

Her mouth hangs open for a second before she closes it, setting her jaw mulishly.

Fine.

"Edith, I'm very sorry that you don't feel you can respect me as a colleague and a human being. I'm sorry you've behaved in such a churlish, petty manner, deliberately disrupting the department and my life. Mostly, I'm sorry for you." *Because you're a miserable old bat who nobody likes and are destined to die without anyone truly mourning for you.* I don't say that, though, because I, at least, know how to be professional. "I have things to do now, so please close the door on your way out."

Her nostrils flare as she sucks in a huge breath, and I'm prepared for her to say something nasty, but instead, she just smirks and leaves. I guess she feels she's won.

Too bad for her that I'm not willing to let this go.

I'm glad she came and spewed her nastiness all over me. Before, I was worn down. Everything seemed hopeless and flat. But I guess I've got a vindictive streak, because now I'm flooded with energy. There's no way I'm letting that bitch win.

THE REST of the day is long. Really long. I send Darryn an email with my recommendation for the interim head of the department, and he sends an email to all staff announcing about the board's new directive, adding the fact that I'm stepping out of the head of department role as an afterthought. I'm grateful to him, and even more grateful to those of my colleagues who immediately replied and cc'd me to say it was a stupid policy and they planned to protest it. Several others sought me out between classes to ask if I'd called the union or a lawyer. One flat-out told me to get Dom involved.

"This school and this town are on JU land. We're all here solely because of JU. He may not officially have any power over us, but we all know if he brings pressure to bear, the board will cave. And it's not like you'd be abusing his influence—this is a ridiculous policy. The town's not that big. Every teacher here has had personal connections to at least one student in some way over the years."

Which is all true, but I'm still not getting Dom involved. Although I will have to tell him about it. Changes like this are public information, and the news is going to spread through the student body. If I don't mention it now, Cara will sometime soon.

But he never needs to know that she was dragged into this.

I wait until the school's done for the day and the students have mostly dispersed to move the few personal items from my office—my ex-office—to my classroom. Then I spend an hour with Emily, who's taking over the department head role. She's spitting mad, insists three times that it's only temporary, and swears that she's not going to make any major decisions without my approval, since she'll be handing the department back to me soon. She also gives me the number of her cousin in Atlanta who's a lawyer.

"I already texted her, and she says it's not her area but one of her colleagues can handle it. Then she texted me again to say her colleague is nearly salivating at the idea. So call her, and at least see what she says."

Truthfully, I've already been thinking about making an appointment to see one of the attorneys in town. I don't know how much experience they'd have with suing for unfair work practices—or would it be discrimination?—since this really isn't that big a town, but they'd probably be able to give me an idea about what my options are.

Not that I really want to sue. But if the policy is clearly and obviously illegal, a letter to the board from a lawyer would probably be enough to make them rescind it, and then Darryn could just reappoint me with a minimum of fuss.

Right as I'm getting ready to go home, the union rep calls me back.

"Sorry it's so late in the day," she says. "I've been in meetings."

I assure her it's no problem and then run down the situation, specifically the new policy.

"Leave it with me" is her instant response. "That's not a reasonable policy, especially not in a town of that size. And especially not when it was introduced in the circumstances you just described. Can you put all that in writing and send it to me? Along with the names of any colleagues who are willing to make a complaint as well. I'm going to chat to the lawyer tomorrow, and we'll probably have a statement for the board by the end of the week." She hesitates. "Your specific situation—"

"Don't worry about that for now," I assure her. "Get the policy repealed, and then if I'm still having problems, we'll see if there's anything you can do." Because fuck knows, it's complicated.

I spend fifteen minutes after we hang up typing an email to her, and bcc those of my colleagues who said they planned to complain.

Then, finally, I go home.

Once I'm in my house, changed into my comfiest sweats, I text Dom and ask him to come over after dinner. I was supposed to go there, but I'd rather not discuss this in front of Cara. I'm sure she and I will talk about it at some stage, but I'm feeling a little raw right now, and I want to tell Dom in private.

He calls me before I even put my phone down.

"Is everything okay?"

"Not really," I say honestly. "I mean, I'm... well, I'm not hurt or sick or anything. But the board made a decision that sucks, and I just feel like wallowing tonight."

He's quiet for a long moment, then says, "Of course I'll come over. I'll bring you some food."

I think about protesting that I can make my own dinner, but I really can't be bothered cooking or even ordering in. "Thank you," I say instead. "Please say hi to Cara for me." I just saw her yesterday, but still.

As soon as the call ends, I drop my phone on the carpet and flop facedown onto the couch, closing my eyes. I'm still there an hour and a half later when I hear a key in the front door.

I don't move when the front door closes. Nor when the keys jingle as they land on the hall table. Not when quiet footsteps cross the room and there's the soft thud of a dish being placed on the coffee table.

But when a warm body sits beside my hip, I roll over and look at him. He looks concerned and a little sad.

"Hey," I whisper.

He smooths my hair back from my forehead. "Hey. I hate seeing you like this."

A tiny smile teases my mouth. "I don't exactly love feeling it." I sit up, scooting back a little so we don't conk heads, but staying close enough to feel his body heat. "It's going to be okay, though. Tonight is for wallowing, and then things are going to change. I'm going to kick ass." I feel stupid as soon as the words are out of my mouth. I just don't say things like that.

Dom just smiles, though, and leans forward to kiss me. "Wanna tell me what happened? Or do we just want to pretend it doesn't exist for tonight?"

As tempting as that is, I shake my head and sigh. "The board's decided that no member of faculty with a personal connection to a student should be in a position to influence or pressure other faculty with regard to that student's grades. So I've been removed as head of the English department."

I actually see the rage light his face. The depth of his caring warms something in me, though I wish I wasn't seeing it for this reason.

"Are you joking?" He leaps to his feet and starts pacing. "Those motherfucking bastards! That can't be legal."

"I'm not sure if it's legal or not, but the general consensus is that it's stupid, especially given we have procedures in place to prevent bias in the case of a personal connection—procedures that have never been complained about." I shrug, feeling the fizz of anger again. "I'll be officially protesting, and so will Darryn, a bunch of other staff, and the union. I'm not just going to accept this."

"Damn right you're not!" He swings around to face me, looking absolutely murderous. "We're going to sue the board and each director personally. We'll drag this through the media until they look so bad, they'll be *begging* to settle."

Whoa.

"That seems a bit extreme." I eye him cautiously. "I'd like to avoid suing if possible. It'd make work really awkward."

"What? You can't be serious," he says incredulously.

"Well… yes. I can't imagine it would be easy to work somewhere after suing them." He can't possibly think it would be, can he?

"No, I mean, you're going to keep working there? For *them*? After they did this to you?" He shakes his head.

"I don't understand. I don't actually work for the board. I work for the school. And of course I'm going to keep working there. It's my job." He thinks I should *quit*? This is not what I expected. I thought he'd want me to fight back. *I* want to fight back.

"They don't deserve to have you there. If they can treat you like this, it's not a healthy work environment."

It's my turn to shake my head. "The people I work with *don't* treat me like this." Well, except for Edith, but I somehow don't think this is the time to mention that. "The people I work with every day, my boss, they're all outraged by this and doing something about it. It's just a couple of random idiots on the board who are causing trouble. I'm not giving up a job I love because of them!" My voice is rising, and I suck in a deep breath to get myself back under control. Are we fighting? Why? I don't understand what's happening here.

He runs a hand through his hair. "We'll find you a new job."

"*A new job?*" What is even happening? "I don't want a new job. I love this job. This is *my* job. Those are *my* students. I've worked hard to shape that department, and I'm not ready to leave it. And even if I was, this isn't exactly a bustling metropolis. High school English teacher jobs aren't exactly thick on the ground in Joyville."

"So we move. You deserve to have a supportive work environment, not jackasses that think they can fuck with you because of who you date."

"*Move?* Are you…? I don't even know…" My brain whirls. What the hell is going through his head? "I don't want to leave Joyville, Dom. I'm happy here. And you certainly can't leave—you're the director."

"So maybe both of us leaving will teach these fuckers to have some respect and stop jerking people around!"

He's pacing again, jerky, angry steps, and I feel like I'm missing something important.

"Look," I begin after a second, "let's leave this for now. I don't want to quit my job—I want back the part they've taken from me. I definitely don't want to leave Joyville. I'm happy here."

He sighs, and the tight knot of tension in my gut starts to unfurl.

"I'm being a dick, aren't I?" he murmurs, coming to

sit beside me again. "I'm sorry, I didn't mean to yell."
He takes my hand, and I squeeze his.

"It's fine. I haven't exactly been calm about this
myself, and at least I knew what was going on. I just
dumped all of this on you tonight."

His thumb traces over the back of my hand. "I still
shouldn't be yelling at *you*. I just… I can't believe you're
still willing to work there. I know you're happy here, but
you could be happy somewhere else. Maybe we should
put some feelers out at some colleges—fuck knows
you're qualified for it, and you'd have better pay and
likely more freedom."

I shake my head again, but this time it's more in
confusion than anything else. He's not wrong about me
having the qualifications—I'm vastly overqualified to be
teaching at high school level, and every once in a while,
I do get inquiries from old colleagues and friends about
whether I'm interested in a position at some college or
other—but I love teaching teenagers. I feel that I make
the most difference at high school level. This is my
chance to get kids hooked on books. To weave the
written word into their lives so completely that it
becomes second nature to them to incorporate reading
—or listening to audiobooks—into the rest of their lives.

And Dom knows that. I've talked about it. He's *teased
me* about it, about my passion for my work. He said he
loves how excited I get when I talk about being a high
school teacher.

"I don't want that," I say plainly. I'm hurt. I…
Maybe he's just reacting still. It's his protective side talking. But part of me, deep down inside, is curling up in a
little ball, because right now, I feel like he doesn't know
me at all.

And worse, it's like he doesn't hear me.

"I just can't handle the thought of you having to work for people who show such little respect for you, who threatened my daughter to get their way."

I open my mouth to tell him—again—that I don't really have anything to do with the board, usually, but then my gut freezes into a huge block of burning cold ice.

"What did you say?" I whisper, and something in my voice must cut through his anger.

He looks at me. "I said they should respect you more. You're worthy of their respect; you're not a pawn for them to play with."

"No." I swallow. "About Cara. What did you say about Cara?"

I see it then. His face sets, but the guilt is there, as clear to read as a neon sign. I pull my hand out of his and stand. It's my turn to pace.

"Oliver—"

I hold up my hand, palm out, warding off his words. "I asked you not to look at the meeting minutes."

"Yeah—"

"You *said* you wouldn't look. You promised me. I asked you not to, and you promised me you wouldn't."

He sucks in a deep breath through his nose, then nods curtly.

"So how did you know they threatened Cara?" I want him to say it. Nothing in my life is the way it should be, and the least he can do is take ownership of his part in that.

Dom looks away, swallows hard. "I read the minutes," he says finally.

I nod. "Yes. Of course." I start to turn away, my thoughts in pieces.

He surges up from the couch and grabs my hand. "Oliver, no. I wasn't going to. I wanted to. I thought about it a lot. But I decided not to. And then you said... the other night. You said you wouldn't let them *hurt* us, and I just couldn't... I can't let anybody hurt you. I wanted to be prepared."

I squeeze my eyes shut. "And were you able to *prepare?*"

The sound he makes is somewhere between a laugh of despair and a sigh. "You know I wasn't. There was nothing I could do. And then I hated myself for breaking my promise."

I pull my hand away from his. I can't think. I can't think, can't get my brain to process this properly. "Not enough to admit it to me."

"I was going to," he insists. "I couldn't keep that from you. But I wanted to wait until everything was resolved. I didn't want to pile it on top of everything else."

My laugh is bitter. "Well, that was a fail. Because now it's piled on this massive heap of shit I'm dealing with, and the worst part is, I don't even know if what you're saying is true. Maybe you would have told me. Maybe you wouldn't. I can't know. I can't know if I can trust your words, because you promised me you wouldn't look at those minutes, and then you did. Worse, you didn't have faith in me to know what I could deal with. If I'd needed your help, if I'd thought for *one second* that Cara's education was actually at risk, I would have told you, Dom. I would have told you and asked for your help. I didn't need your help. There was nothing you could do."

"I know. I'm sorry. So sorry. I was wro—"

"You went behind my back because you didn't believe I could handle this. You broke a promise to me. And the way you've been talking tonight, about me quitting and looking for a job at a college… it's like you don't even know who I am or care what I want."

"That's not true!" He looks frantic now, his words vehement, but everything is just too much, too loud. All I wanted tonight was some comfort from my boyfriend, and he's made things *worse*.

"What part's not true?"

"I just want you to have a job where nobody will screw with you and Cara because of me."

"And that's more important than what I want?"

"No, I…" His mouth is open, but he can't seem to find the right words.

"Fuck you, Dom. Fuck you for thinking you know best. Fuck you for not valuing me enough to respect what *I* want and keep your promises to me. I deserve better than that." My heart is broken, gone, ripped clear out of my chest and shredded to a million pieces. I'm not even angry anymore—just empty and cold. "Get out. We're done."

"Oliver—"

"No. Just stay away from me." I walk calmly down the hall to the downstairs bathroom and lock myself in. I don't know why. I just need to be somewhere else.

For a long moment, I hear nothing. Then loud, fast footsteps stride through the house, and the front door closes hard. It's not quite a slam, but it's not gentle, either.

And I'm alone.

My knees give way, and I slump to the floor, right there in the middle of the bathroom, the tile cold through the worn fleece of my sweatpants.

How could all this have happened? A week ago, I was so happy. I had a job I loved. I had a man in my life who I was ready to say I loved. I thought… I thought I'd found my forever guy. We haven't—hadn't—been together that long, really, but it all felt so right. I was sure it was… *it*. I was thinking about suggesting we move in together when Cara left for college—planning long weekends up to visit her next year. We were talking about having a cookout at my place for Dom's colleagues once the weather gets better.

How could he so completely overlook my feelings? My dreams?

I slide sideways until I'm lying on the cold floor and let the hot tears trickle down my face.

FIFTEEN

Dom

I don't know what to do.

What the fuck just happened?

What the fuck?

I put my turn signal on automatically, take the corner, then just as I have the last eight times, I slow as I pass Oliver's house. There's still no sign of him—no silhouette in the front room. I can't keep circling the block like this, but I can't leave either.

I don't know what to do.

My phone ringing through the speakers startles me enough that the car swerves slightly, and I make myself pull over, breathing deeply. I answer the call out of habit, then wish I hadn't. I don't want to talk to anyone.

"Dom?" It's Dimi, his concerned voice filling the car and reverberating through my head. "Listen, my mom just called. Oliver called her today, and she's been trying to call him back, but he's not answering. She, uh, she said she heard… uh, something about him… having trouble with the school board?" Dimi's picking his words carefully, which means he knows but isn't sure if I do and doesn't want to breach a confidence.

"We broke up," I say, the words heavy. "He… he told me to get out."

"Fuck. Uh…" His voice fades a little, as though he's pulled the phone away and is talking to someone else. "Call Mom, will you, and tell her he's probably not going to answer tonight, but she should leave a message." Another voice—Jason?—says something, and then Dimi's back, talking to me again. "Dom, where are you? Are you home? Is Cara there?"

I look around. "I'm in my car."

"Okay. Are you safe to drive? I can come and get you."

Like a switch flipping, reason floods back, and I shake my head. "I can drive, Dimi. But thanks. I'm okay."

He scoffs. "Yeah, I don't think so. Come over. Do you remember how to get here?"

I hesitate, because really I just want to go home and crawl into bed and try to get the noise in my head to stop so I can work out what happened and where everything went so wrong. But the reality is that Cara is at home, and if I crawl into bed before eight o'clock, she's going to freak out and I'll have to tell her what happened. In fact, if I go home now, so early, when I'm supposed to be spending the evening with Oliver, she's going to freak out and I'll have to tell her what happened. I know I'll have to tell her eventually anyway, but not now, when I barely understand it all myself.

"I remember," I say, putting the car in gear and carefully pulling back onto the road. Dimi's good with problem solving. Maybe he'll be able to explain how everything went to shit so fast.

———————

TWENTY MINUTES LATER, I'm sitting on Dimi and Jason's couch, staring at a cup of coffee with a healthy slug of whiskey in it—because as Dimi said, I have to go home to my daughter, so I can't get blind drunk, but this will at least take the edge off.

"Do you want to talk about it?" Jason asks gently. Dimi makes a tiny noise, probably because he has a million questions and here's Jason giving me an out.

I sigh. "Kind of. Dimi, you said Oliver called your mom today?"

They exchange glances, and then Dimi says, "Yeah. She thinks it has to do with the school board?" He says it like a question, fishing to see what I know.

I nod, then run down the whole situation for them, starting with Oliver being called to the monthly board meeting and finishing with me leaving his place. There's a stunned silence when I'm done.

"I'm so sorry, Dom," Jason says softly. I lift my gaze to meet his.

"Why? I'm the asshole here. I—" I stop, fighting for control. "He's right. I didn't stop to think of what he wanted. But I never intended..." I can't finish. It's all still muddled in my head, but I can see where I went wrong. I was so determined to protect Oliver, to fix things for him, that I forgot he's capable of protecting himself. I forgot that he never asked me to protect him. And I forgot to take his needs into account.

"You did an asshole thing, but you're not an

asshole," Jason corrects. "The fact that you can see you were wrong proves that."

"That doesn't mean you won't have to grovel," Dimi adds. "A lot."

I shake my head. "He was pretty clear. I don't think groveling will help. And I don't want to solidify my status as an asshole by ignoring his wishes and not leaving him alone." I do really want him to know I'm sorry, though.

"That is so fucked-up," Dimi mutters.

"Why don't we come back to this," Jason says diplomatically. "I'm sure everything's a bit raw right now."

He's right, but my brain is stuck on what Dimi said. "You don't think I should respect his wishes?"

Dimi rolls his eyes. "Of course you should respect his wishes, but you also need to consider how upset he was when he told you to leave him alone. At the very least, you need to apologize. You hurt him, and you need to show him that you know you were wrong and that his feelings right now are justified."

I like the sound of this—it's definitely better than sitting on my ass and doing nothing to fix this whole dumpster fire—but…

"But wouldn't I be making things worse? I mean, he's mad partly because I ignored his wants and his feelings, and so I'm going to ignore his wants again to tell him he's right to be mad?" I take a slug of the coffee, and my eyes cross. Fuck, Dimi's got a heavy hand with the whiskey.

He huffs, one of those I-can't-believe-you're-this-stupid sounds, and I prepare to feel like an idiot.

"That's why you do it on his terms. Send him a text or an email saying you're sorry, that he was right, and that if and when he's ready, you'd like to apologize in person, no strings attached. And then you leave him alone until he reaches out to you."

"*If* he reaches out to me," I mutter, but he's right. This is the least intrusive way of letting Oliver know I'm willing to grovel. The ball needs to stay in his court, because I'm the one who fucked up, but he needs to know that ball exists. "Not tonight," I decide, because Jason's right. I'm raw right now, and Oliver probably is too. And the fact is, he may not ever be able to forgive me for acting as though he wasn't a person with feelings and a brain. He said he couldn't trust that I was telling him the truth because I broke my promise, and I can't blame him for that. This wasn't a little white lie. He asked me not to do something, something that was important to him, and I did it anyway. Even if he forgives me—*please, let him forgive me*—anytime I ever make a promise in future, a part of each of us will remember. That's a big thing to overcome.

"I should have listened to Luke."

"Probably," Dimi agrees without missing a beat. "He's a pretty level-headed guy. Although he makes mistakes too, so maybe think about it before blindly following his advice."

"What does your mom know about what's going on with the board?" I ask abruptly, because I'm done talking about the ruins of my relationship.

Dimi raises an eyebrow but goes along with my change of subject. "By now, everything. According to her, there were some rumors over the weekend that some of the board members weren't happy about something that was under discussion. Then she got a call from Marcus from the library this morning. He told her that if she were still on the board, she'd be very unhappy, and that if she wanted her grandkids to be attending schools where teachers are judged by their ability to educate rather than because of an outdated political hierarchy, she should be ready to protest."

I haven't had a lot of contact with Dimi's mom, but even I know that's like feeding trees to a forest fire. "So, Marcus from the library is a smart man." I'm pretty sure I've met him a couple of times.

Jason snorts. "He's pretty cool. And of course, Sascha immediately started making calls, trying to find out what was going on. It didn't take her long to get the whole story."

"And then Oliver called her?" I ask. I'm sure I remember Dimi saying that.

He nods. "He had to leave a message because she was working, but the fact that he's reaching out to her today is a pretty good indication that he's looking for community support."

"Yeah." I turn it over in my head. "I've been meaning to ask… why isn't your mom on the town council? Or the school board?" Or in the White House?

Dimi shrugs. "She used to be on the school board, but she resigned a couple years after Brody graduated. She said she wanted to concentrate more on her business and on the grandkids. She's been asked several times to run for town council—I remember people asking when I was a kid, even—but she's always said it would take too much time away from her family. My take is that she enjoys being the committee queen without the restrictions she'd have if she was 'official.'"

"She certainly gets away with a lot more this way than she would if she had to play politics," Jason muses.

"Either way, she definitely doesn't like this policy and has already started the ball rolling to protest it. The school board should brace for a mob of unhappy parents."

My phone rings, and adrenaline races through me so fast, I get dizzy. Could it be Oliver? I fumble it out of my pocket, but the name on the screen is Luke's. Disappointment hits hard. For a second, I think about ignoring it, but Luke generally doesn't call me out of work hours. It might be important.

Even if it isn't, it will be a distraction.

I swipe the screen and lift the phone to my ear. "Hey."

"Dom, what the fuck? Mila just got a call from a friend who said Oliver's been fired?" I can hear Mila in the background, her voice raised—is she crying? It sounds like she's crying.

"He hasn't been fired," I assure Luke immediately. "But he's no longer head of the English department."

I hear him repeating that to Mila, who stops yelling, and a second later, Luke comes back and says, "Is this to do with the meeting from last week? What happened?"

"Someone made a bullshit complaint about him potentially being biased toward Cara, and then when that was proved groundless, they insisted that no teacher with a personal connection to a student should be in a position of authority over other teachers, or some shit like that. The board implemented this policy, and Oliver got demoted because of it."

"He got demoted because he's dating a student's father? But he doesn't even teach Cara," Luke protested, and my eyes go wide.

"Shit—Cara doesn't know. I have to call her before

one of her friends does." Fuck. I can't believe I underestimated the gossip circuit in this town yet again.

"I think you're too late," Luke says. "Mila just answered her phone and said Cara's name. Hold on." I hear him ask Mila who she's talking to, and then he tells me, "Sorry, Dom. She's heard. She tried calling Oliver, but when he didn't pick up—"

"She called Mila. Could you tell her to hang up and I'll call her now?" I should just go home, and I will, but I want to check in and make sure she's okay first.

There's another relayed conversation between Luke, Mila, and Cara, and then Luke comes back, a note of laughter in his voice as he says, "She wants me to tell you not to bother calling. She'll be on the phone to all her friends and classmates, letting them know what happened and organizing a meeting so they can plan a protest."

A laugh bursts from me, and I'm swamped with pride. My daughter is so amazing. "That sounds about right," I reply, then look over at Dimi. "Cara's planning a protest."

He grins and grabs his phone. "I'll text her and put her in touch with Mom."

In my ear, Luke says, "She also asked me to have you pass her love to Oliver and to tell him everyone is, and I quote, 'super pissed off' about this. How's he doing? Is there anything Grant and I can do for him?"

The breath freezes in my lungs, and I make a sound I can't describe. Fuck. Fuck. I need to tell Cara that Oliver and I broke up.

"Dom?" There's concern in Luke's voice again, and I force words through my too-tight throat.

"Can you go somewhere Mila can't hear?"

There's a long pause.

"Sure. Just a sec." He says something muffled, then I hear movement, the background noise fading, and a moment later, he says, "Okay, it's just me and Grant."

"Oliver and I broke up. He broke up with me." It erupts from me before I can think about what I want to say, and I hear a sharply indrawn breath through the phone. Jason reaches out and puts a hand on my arm, and while I'm grateful for the contact, for the assurance that I'm not completely alone, I'm also too raw and sensitive right now.

Fuck, feelings are hard.

"Where are you?" Luke asks finally.

"At Dimi and Jason's. Dimi called right after... after I... I was in the car." I'm pretty sure that sentence doesn't make sense, but he seems to get what I was trying to say.

"That's good," he says. "Uh, do you want to talk about it? What happened?"

Dimi's phone chimes, and he picks it up and flicks the button on the side to switch it to silent before replying. I'm about 95 percent sure it's either Cara, about the protest, or Grant, checking how I *really* am. Either option makes me feel a little better. Cara was right to force me to make friends.

Even if I've just lost my best friend.

"I... Do you remember what we talked about last week?" I don't want to tell it all again.

He hesitates for a second, then says, "The meeting minutes? You looked?"

"Yeah. And I said some other stupid stuff. He-He wasn't wrong to feel this way. I fucked up."

"I doubt that makes either of you feel better right

now. Do you want to stay with Dimi and Jase tonight, just wallow? I can go pick up Cara, and she and Mila can have a weeknight slumber party or whatever."

I'm so tempted. If you ask Cara, she's old enough to stay alone overnight anyway, and she might be right—after all, in just a few months she'll be moving to another state for college. But I've never been able to leave her on her own all night, not yet, and she's always just rolled her eyes and laughed about it. If I go home now, she's going to have a million questions. There's no way she'll miss that I'm not exactly myself. How do I explain to my seventeen-year-old daughter that I'm a total asshole? And she'd probably welcome the chance to workshop protest ideas with Mila tonight.

On the other hand, she's going to go to school tomorrow and begin organizing this protest. There's absolutely no chance that she won't seek Oliver out to tell him in person that he has her support. I need to tell her that we broke up. I can't dump that burden on him.

"Thanks, but I need to talk to her tonight, before she goes to school tomorrow." I rub my forehead as Luke makes a sympathetic noise.

"The offer stands, anytime you want a night off. Call if you need anything in the meantime, and I'll see you at work tomorrow."

God. Work. That means I have to make my brain function. "Thanks, Luke."

We end the call, and I look at Dimi. "Cara or Grant?"

He has the grace to flush. "Both, actually. And then Derek. Grant texted him, but he'd already heard about the school situation and was trying to call you."

I shake my head. "How did Derek hear?" He doesn't have a teenager.

Dimi shrugs. "Not sure. But it's going around town, so…"

Yeah. Damn gossip.

Oh god, it's not going to be long before everyone knows Oliver and I aren't together anymore.

They must see the horror on my face, because Jason says, "Let's just take one thing at a time. I know you want to go home to Cara, but is there anything we can do for you?"

I shake my head again. "I think I just need to sit with this tonight. I… I really want to take charge of this whole thing with the school board, but Oliver specifically asked me not to interfere. I should try to respect at least some of his wishes, since I ran roughshod over everything else."

"Let him handle it," Dimi agrees. "But remember that you're a parent at that school and you do have some input in that capacity. You're not just the director."

"I know it's hard not to step in when you know you could fix things—or at least help them along," Jason adds. "But this really is his fight. You're going to have to live with that."

Damn them for being reasonable. I lift my almost forgotten mug and gulp down the cold coffee, shuddering because of the temperature and the strong alcohol.

"Thanks, guys. I guess it's time to go home."

CARA MEETS me two feet from the front door. Her face is alight with indignation and determination as she expounds on the stupidity and unfairness of this new policy.

I close my eyes and take a deep breath, and she stops midsentence. When I open my eyes, she's watching me warily.

"What happened?"

"It's fine," I assure her, then change my mind. Empty platitudes won't help. "No, it's not. Nobody's injured," I settle on.

"Dad, you're scaring me." Her eyes are wide now, and it kills me that I've put that look on her face— almost as much as it kills me how upset and disappointed she's going to be in a few minutes.

"There's nothing to be scared about, I swear. Uh, maybe we should go sit down." I look toward the couch, but Cara's shaking her head.

"Dad, please just tell me what's going on."

I wince. "I messed up." Fuck, do I give her details? I'm doing this all wrong. She's never liked anyone I've dated this much before—not since her mom, anyway.

She's watching me expectantly, and I see it—the moment she realizes what I'm not saying. Her face falls, and honestly, it's a kick in the gut to see how devastated she looks. Her face is the mirror to how I feel.

"You and Oliver broke up?" she whispers, and hearing someone else say it is so much worse than saying it myself.

I force a nod.

"*Why?*" It's torn from her. "You're so good together. And he needs you right now. What happened?"

"I messed up." It's all I can say. "I… I messed up."

She rubs her palms over her face, then looks at me again, suddenly pale. "You... you didn't... You're not seeing someone else, are you?"

A sound bursts from my throat that might have been a laugh under other circumstances. "No. No, I didn't cheat. I broke a promise—something that was important to him. And I wasn't as supportive of him as I should have been."

It looks like she wants to ask for more information, but instead, she steps forward and wraps her arms around my waist. "I'm so sorry, Dad. Maybe once you've both had time to process, you'll get a second chance."

I almost laugh for real this time. She sounds so adult and yet so naïve. "Yeah, maybe," I say, because what the hell else is there to say?

"Come and sit down." She steers me toward the couch, and it's only as I'm sinking into it, feeling like utter crap, that I see the list on the coffee table. Even from here, I can tell it's a to-do list of what's needed to organize a student protest.

She snatches it up. "Uh. Does it bother you...?"

I shake my head, reach out, and pull her close. Planting a kiss on the top of her head, I say, "No, it doesn't bother me. Don't change your plans because of me. Oliver deserves your support—he deserves to get his job back."

"Good. Because I wouldn't have stopped, just made sure to do it when you weren't around."

A smile stretches my lips. It's more of an instinctive reaction than anything else. I don't feel happy, or even amused. But Cara said something cute, so I smiled.

Leaning her head against my shoulder, she asks, "Are

they doing this to him because of me?" My entire body tenses, and she hurries on, "I mean, I know they are—I'm a student and he's dating my dad—but it just seems weird that it's suddenly come up now. Is it because I'm too opinionated at school?" There's a note of vulnerability in her voice, and I *hate* it. How dare anyone make my baby feel this way?

"No," I say firmly. "They're doing this for a lot of reasons. Some of it is me—if Oliver had been dating another parent, someone whose job wasn't as high profile, this probably wouldn't have happened. It could also be because of some... personal issues between Oliver and one of his colleagues. Someone who jumped on the first excuse they could find to cause trouble for him." She doesn't need to know more about that. "But the only people at fault are the closed-minded fuckheads who think they have the right to control other people's lives. You're just the tool they used."

She sighs. "Great. Well, lucky for them, they'll get to hear exactly what I think of that." She hesitates. "Um... I don't want to rub salt in the wound or anything, but if you guys are broken up, doesn't that resolve the issue? I mean, if they demoted him because he was dating you and you're my dad, and now he's not dating you..."

I have to swallow several times before I can speak. She's right, and I want Oliver to have his job back and be happy, but if he uses our breakup to get it, that means we're never getting back together, doesn't it?

"I guess it would," I finally say. "It would be up to Oliver to tell the board."

"We'll still go ahead with the protest," she muses. "The policy is wrong. Just because it might not have an effect on anyone right now doesn't mean it won't in future."

Jesus fucking Christ, my heart is bleeding. Not have an effect? It's having an effect on me. That might be partly my fault, but if the board had just left everything alone, my asshole tendencies probably wouldn't have risen to the fore. Not yet, anyway.

We sit there for a while longer. I'm exhausted in a way that I know means stress rather than actual physical tiredness, but if I go to bed, I'll have to close my eyes and see the night replay in my head.

How could I have fucked things up so badly?

SIXTEEN

Oliver

_____

I drag myself out of bed when the alarm goes off, purposely keeping my mind blank as I shuffle to the kitchen for coffee. I can smell it, which means someone's made it. Jaiden. Jaiden's made it. He turned up last night—I still don't know why—used his key to get in, and pounded on the bathroom door until I scraped myself up off the floor and unlocked it. Then he made me hot tea with something medicinal in it and crawled into bed with me until I fell asleep.

"Here." He shoves a mug of coffee at me now, and I take it and slump at the kitchen table while he puts bread in the toaster.

"Thanks." I take a sip. "Why are you here?" I honestly didn't mean it to come out that blunt, but now that the words are out, I don't have the energy to explain what I intended.

Fortunately, he seems to get it. "Grant Davis called me last night. He said you and Dom had broken up and suggested I check on you."

"Fucking gossip," I hiss, and he starts, possibly at the venom in my tone.

"I don't think it's gossip," he protests. "Nobody else seems to know. Dom probably went to his friends, and they wanted to make sure you were okay. Which is a good thing, because you weren't."

"I was fine." I don't want to think about it, much less talk about it. This is my own fault—if I hadn't asked, he wouldn't have brought it up. Well, maybe.

"You weren't fine." He gets the butter and jam from the fridge and opens a drawer in search of a knife. "You were almost in shock."

"Don't exaggerate. Shock is an actual medical condition. People miscategorize feeling shocked as being *in shock* all the time, and it's incorrect."

"Oh, sorry. Next time I find my best friend huddled on a bathroom floor, shivering and clammy and unable to speak, I'll make sure to use the correct expression." He slams the drawer, the sarcastic edge to his words almost as sharp as the bang it makes. "Jesus, Oliver, I nearly called an ambulance."

I make myself take a breath, hold it, and then let it out. "I'm sorry. I didn't mean to worry you."

He sighs. "No, it's not your fault. I'm just glad you're doing better this morning." He hesitates. "Do you want me to call in for you? Nobody would blame you if—"

"I'd blame me." My voice is sharp, and I deliberately moderate it. "I have classes. And I need to speak to some people about getting this idiotic policy revoked." His silence speaks volumes, and I look up. "What?"

He shrugs a little. "Nothing. Just… if you and Dom have broken up, then all you need to do is tell Darryn, and he'll give you the head of department job back in a heartbeat."

The world freezes around me. My heartbeat pounds loudly in my ears, speeding up until I have to breathe deeply and slowly to regulate it.

Oh my god. Dom and I aren't together anymore.

I knew. Of course I knew—I was the one who told him to leave. But I didn't realize… this means he's not… we're not…

My chest hurts.

"Oliver?" Jaiden's voice is sharp, and I realize I'm pressing a hand to my chest. I let it drop.

"I'm fine," I assure him before he calls 911 and tells them I'm having a heart attack. "It's just… anxiety, I guess." I can't believe Dom and I are over.

I can't believe he wasn't who I thought he was. That he lied to me and, worse, never really understood me. Thought I'd walk away from my job and my life instead of fighting for them.

I push that aside and focus on what Jaiden said: if Dom and I aren't together, then the new policy doesn't apply to me.

"Uh… keep it to yourself, will you? That Dom and I split up. And could you text Grant and ask that he and Dom's other friends not mention it either?" It's on the tip of my tongue to ask him to give Dom the same message, but I've got more spine than that.

Jaiden studies me. "Sure. Of course. But… you're not going to…?"

I shake my head. "No. This policy is wrong. I don't want people being distracted from that. I want that job back because the school board has seen the error of its ways and revoked the policy, not because I happen to be single now. Something like this could happen again later —then what?"

Jaiden snorts. "You're such an idealist." He hurries on as I open my mouth to argue. "But, yes, fine—I'll keep it to myself and text Grant. Let's teach the board a lesson." He passes me the toast.

"Thank you," I tell him, and I don't just mean for breakfast. Waking up on the hard, cold bathroom floor wouldn't have been fun.

"You're welcome. I'm going to run home to change. See you at work?"

I nod, and a minute later, he's gone. Leaving me with hot toast, coffee, an empty house, and an aching heart.

I WAIT until I'm at school and there's only five minutes until my first class before texting Dom. My hands are shaking. Part of me wants to delete his contact from my phone, then also smash the phone to bits and get a new one. Another part wants to print out every message he sent me and bind them into a book I can keep forever. The most sensible—and yet painful—part suggests I tell him how angry I am but that I want to try to work through it. I'm not ready for that, so instead I settle for sending a text that will allow me to focus on salvaging my career.

Oliver: Please don't tell anyone we're not together anymore. I'd like to deal with the board without any additional distractions.

There. To the point and polite. And now I can turn off my phone and put it in a drawer and not check it until class is over.

It buzzes in my hand, and I squeeze my eyes shut. Of course I'm that unlucky, and he had his phone at hand. Now what? Do I read his reply and potentially have it weighing on my mind during class, or do I ignore it until later and definitely have it weighing on my mind during class?

A few early students come in and call greetings. I smile and say hello and stab the screen with my thumb, because I won't be able to do my class justice if I don't read this text.

Dom: Of course. Cara and some friends know, but I'll text them right now and ask them not to tell anyone. We all support you completely in this. I'm so very sorry for the way I've behaved. You were right. I should never have looked at those minutes, and I should have thought about what you would want and not about what makes me feel better. I'm sorry, and I hope that one day you'll allow me to apologize again in person.

I blink hard, then turn off my phone and shove it in my desk drawer.

By the time the end of the school day approaches, I'm wrecked. People are reacting more strongly—and faster—to the board's new policy than I expected. I've received numerous calls and emails from parents, both present and past, offering support and advising that they've contacted the board to lodge their protest. It's gratifying and heartwarming, but I won't lie—I'm surprised. I knew I was liked as a teacher and a member of the community, but I thought it was more of a general thing—it shames me to say it, but I didn't think people would actually go out of their way to support me on something that didn't impact them directly. I know better now.

I spent my lunch break on the phone with first Emily's lawyer cousin's colleague, who laid out my options pretty clearly, and then with Sascha Weston, who advised me she was circulating a petition but also encouraging people to contact the board directly. She also said there was a student protest being planned and that she'd been asked if I would address a few words. While it really warms my heart to think of my students stepping up like this, it would be completely inappropriate for me to even attend, much less speak, so I politely declined but told her to pass on my thanks. And then somehow, I volunteered to be part of the spring fundraising drive for the town's free clinic.

Only Sascha could call to offer support and get something out of it. I don't mind, though—it's definitely a worthy cause, and maybe I should be giving back a bit more to this town.

So when the last bell finally rings and my students all leave in a chattering mass, I let my spine unbend and for just a moment allow my misery to take me over.

"Oliver? I mean, Mr. Jeffries?"

I stiffen, because I know that voice. Turning toward the door, I force a smile to my lips.

"Hey, Cara."

None of this is her fault. None of this makes me any less fond of her. Part of me had already started thinking of her as my future stepdaughter, and I liked the idea of having a grown-up stepkid. Losing that future—losing contact with Cara—crushes another part of my already ripped-up heart.

She smiles back, but it's tremulous and not at all like

her usual beam of energy. Her eyes are a little glassy, and she pauses to close them and suck in a deep breath before she comes to lean against my desk.

"This sucks," she whispers.

"I— Yes. It does." I don't know what to say, what Dom told her. Obviously that we're broken up, but does she think it was a mutual thing? I wouldn't blame him if that's what he told her. Being a parent is hard enough without having to tell your child you did something wrong.

"He's sorry, you know. He knows he was wrong, and he regrets being a dick."

My eyebrows shoot up, and she waves a hand.

"Yeah, language, I know. Sorry. I just wanted you to know I know he was in the wrong. And he called me this morning and said to keep—keep everything to myself, and I have. Nobody will hear it from me."

"Thank you. I appreciate that, Cara. And I'm… I'm sorry things have worked out this way." I don't know what to say about Dom, about the fact that he's obviously told Cara at least part of what happened.

"We both support you however you want to fight the board. If there's anything we can do, just let me know. Dad says he won't step in unless you want him to, because he doesn't want to screw up your plans by being heavy-handed." The tiny snort she gives at the end of that sentence makes me chuckle. We both know Dom's primary setting is heavy-handed.

She meets my gaze, and her smile this time is a little more natural but sad. "I'm going to miss you. You're so good for him. I really wanted him to have someone when I go, and you were better for him than anybody I could have dreamed up."

My throat is too tight to answer, and I'm swamped with relief when Jaiden knocks on the open door.

"Sorry to interrupt. Oliver, are you ready to go?"

I don't know where he thinks we're going, but Cara takes that as her cue to leave, and so I'm grateful for the interruption.

"Anyway, thanks. I'll see you around." She smiles at us both and then disappears into the hallway. I slump back over my desk.

"Rough day?" Jaiden asks, and I nod without looking at him. "Come on, then. Back to your place. You can tell me all about it while I make dinner."

"I have a stack of assignments to grade," I say, although I'm not sure what that's got to do with him cooking.

"You'll get to them."

I'm not in the mood to argue, so I pack up my stuff and follow him out to the staff parking lot, where I get in my car and follow him to my house. While I go to change clothes, he installs himself in my guest bedroom —where he'd been staying until not that long ago—then we meet in the kitchen, both of us with piles of grading.

"Want to tell me about it?" he asks, and I realize that he doesn't know any of the details yet. I haven't had a chance to tell him. Because it's been less than twenty-four hours, not the million days it feels like.

I give him a rundown, fiddling idly with a red pen. It's painful to say it all out loud, but at the same time, kind of freeing. He listens without interrupting, and when I'm done, he sighs.

"I never would have expected Dom to be such a fuckhead."

I laugh, the sound bursting from me unintentionally.

"Me either." I clear my throat. "He sent me an apology text." I unlock my phone and hand it over so he can see.

"Well, at least he's aware that he's a fuckhead." Jaiden passes the phone back. "That's kind of a relief."

I say nothing.

"Hey." He puts his hand on my arm. "Oliver, you're allowed to be angry and upset about this. He fucked up. He hurt you. The fact that he's aware and sorry doesn't mean you have to forgive him. Let yourself feel what you're feeling, and if sometime down the track you want to let him grovel in person, text him. But if you never want to see him again, or if you want to curse his name every Sunday, or whatever, that's fine."

I smile because I know that's what he wants. "I just want to get through this situation at work. I don't have the energy to give to anything else."

He nods. "Then that's what you do. Until then, Dominic Hurst doesn't exist. And he can continue not existing after that too, if that's what you want."

If only that made it hurt less.

DESPITE MY FEARS, the end of the week rolls around a lot faster than I expected. On Friday afternoon, more than half of the students walk out of class to protest in front of the school. I'm shocked by the number—I knew it would get a lot of attention, especially since some teenagers will grab any excuse to miss class, but I didn't think that many would participate. I watch from Jaiden's classroom window, since all our students for the last class of the day seem to be out there. None of them turned up to class, anyway.

Cara and her cohorts did a good job. The rally isn't rowdy, with a lot of the seniors circulating through the crowd and quick to convene on any student or group who look to be getting a little too excited. They have signs and are chanting slogans, and they've attracted both local and regional press. Jamie is talking to them while Cara stands beside him. He gestures to her a few times, and she makes several comments, seemingly in response to questions, but mostly she lets him take the lead. It's not like her, and I wonder about it.

"Oh, good, the viewing area is already in use," a voice says, and I turn to see Lindy coming into the room and crossing to where we stand by the window. "I spent the last twenty minutes trying to convince myself it would be a very bad idea to go out there, even though I really want to know what's going on. And then I remembered these amazing things called windows and that some of them overlooked the front of the building." She scans the crowd. "Is it wrong that I'm really proud of these kids right now? I mean, look at that." She waves at the scene outside. "That's as well planned and executed as anything an experienced adult could do."

I open my mouth to answer, but she's still talking.

"Hey, they got a great press turnout. And I'll bet this is already all over social media. That'll put the pressure on the board." She tips her head and studies the small group talking to the press. "It's easy to underestimate what a smart girl Cara is, isn't it? I'll admit, a few times I've gotten frustrated with her questioning everything and wondered if she just wants attention, but look at her now."

I look again. Jamie's talking again, and Cara is

nodding along but saying nothing. "What do you mean?"

"Well, I don't know this for sure, but I'd say she asked Jamie to be spokesperson because she knew that if she did it, someone would spin it to sound like she planned this whole thing just because you're her dad's boyfriend. This way, she's just part of the narrative—a student whose family has been victimized, sure, but the point of the rally is the policy, not her story."

Fuck me, she's right.

I look at the group again, with new eyes. I know exactly what Cara is capable of, and I still underestimated her.

"I'm sure Jamie's had a huge part to play in organizing this," Lindy continues, "but we all know Cara would probably have been a better spokesperson. The optics of both of them being there—both top students, both highly involved in extracurricular activities, both popular and sure to go on to good colleges next year—are fantastic. These are students who genuinely care about their school and the education it provides."

"You've spent way too much time thinking about this," Jaiden tells her, but he's studying the rally with new interest. "I am proud of them, though."

We watch as Darryn exits the school and heads toward the cluster of journalists. "What's he doing?" I wonder.

Lindy smirks. "I heard that the students asked if he could make a statement to the press on behalf of the school and the board."

"And he's going to?" Jaiden's voice reflects my shock.

"The same little birdy told me that he called the board and told them it would be better to make a calm statement that puts the situation in the best light than to look like they were hiding from the press." The little birdy has to be Maria, who's privy to everything that happens in the administration wing. But surely the board couldn't be so stupid as to have agreed? Darryn's made his position on this very clear—why would they think he was going to say something to the media that wouldn't support that?

And what *is* he going to say?

"I don't suppose any of those cameras are streaming live, are they?" Jaiden asks. "I'd really like to hear this bit."

"Unlikely," I murmur, but Lindy has already pulled out her phone.

"Let's see, who's out there... ooh, wait, does that look like Sarah Stromburgh is recording?" We all lean closer to the window.

"Maybe she's posting to social media?" Jaiden suggests. "What do they all use these days?"

"It'd be too long for Tik Tok, wouldn't it? Or was that Snapchat that had to have short posts? Can you even do a live post on Tik Tok?"

I look at her like she's speaking Greek. I've heard of Tik Tok, of course, but that's the sum total of my knowledge—that it exists.

"I'll try Instagram," she decides. "That's more likely than Facebook." Sure enough, a few seconds later she lets out a triumphant cry. "Got it."

We crowd around her phone, and she turns the volume right up. The angle is a bit off to the side, but it's still clear who's speaking—and what they're saying.

"...our school principal, Darryn Singh, has kindly agreed to make a statement on behalf of the school and the Joyville Public Schools Board," Jamie is saying just as Darryn comes to a halt beside him. "Principal Singh?"

Darryn smiles calmly. "Thank you, Jamie. First, I'd like to acknowledge the amazing job the students have done here today. While I wish they didn't feel they needed to protest, I am grateful for and admiring of the way they have done it. They should be proud that they've been able to get their message across."

Jamie and Cara both grin but say nothing.

"The Joyville Public Schools Board made a decision early this week that it feels will best serve the students and staff at Joyville High School."

There's a beat while everyone waits for him to continue, but he's seemingly done.

"What the heck?" Lindy mutters.

Then the questions begin. They're not as clear, but one is shouted loudly enough to drown out the others.

"Are you saying that this decision *only* affects the high school?"

"Oh," Jaiden says.

I hadn't thought about that.

Darryn says, "I'm only aware of policies that relate to my school. I can't speak as to any of the others."

"Mr. Singh, did the board make this decision because of an incident of favoritism?"

Darryn's eyes light with fervor. "No. The school has several excellent policies in place to prevent favoritism in the event that a teacher and student have a personal connection outside the school. These policies, which are available for public review via the school's website, have been implemented many times over the years. To my knowledge, we have never had a sustained complaint of favoritism."

"Never?" someone says skeptically. "Not even before the policies were introduced?"

"The first principal of this school had three of his own children enrolled," Darryn says with a placid smile. "He was the one who wrote those policies, as he wanted it to be clear that the school was run completely above-board. They've been reviewed regularly over the years, and I believe some wording has been tweaked in line with state and federal law changes, but as far as I'm aware, they are the same policies and have been upheld."

"So why this new policy?"

"Oooohhhh," Lindy says. "This'll be good."

"Shh," Jaiden hisses, his attention glued to the screen.

"The board has made a decision it feels will best serve the students and staff," Darryn says.

There's a flurry of whys and demands for more information. Darryn keeps his calm smile the whole time, then adds, "I can't speak to the board's decision-making process."

One of the journalists changes tack, asking, "How do you feel about the fact that this new policy forced one of your staff, Oliver Jeffries, to be removed from his job?"

"First, I'd like to clarify that Mr. Jeffries is still teaching at this school but is no longer head of the English department. He is an excellent teacher, was an excellent department head, and we're lucky to have him. I deeply regret that he is unable to continue in that role."

"So this policy is the only reason for his employment change?"

"Yes." The blunt way Darryn says it gives me warm feelings inside.

The resulting barrage of questions comes fast and thick and is basically a mess of sound, but as it begins to settle, someone calls, "Are you saying the board implemented an unnecessary policy that forced a job change on a longtime employee despite the fact that it's to the school's detriment?"

"He can't answer this one," I mutter. "He's already pushing his luck."

"The board has made a decision it feels will best serve students and staff," he repeats, and this time there's no mistaking the slightly mocking tone. "Thank you for your time."

As he retreats back toward the school, Jamie steps in and thanks the journalists for coming, then asks if there are any other questions. Lindy closes the app, and we look at each other.

"Darryn's screwed," Jaiden says, and even though it's what I'm thinking, my stomach still sinks. I didn't want anyone dragged down with me.

Lindy shakes her head. "They can't fire him. Not after giving him permission to speak to the media. And he stuck to the whole 'best decision' thing pretty stringently."

"Yeah, but everything else he said," I protest. "He made it sound pretty clear that he thinks the board is being discriminatory and dumb."

"Well, they are. But if you think about it, he really just defended the school's policies and then answered questions about you honestly. He can argue that if he'd answered any other way, it would have opened him and the school up to a civil suit for slander." She shakes her head again. "Darryn's a clever cookie. The kids' work here would maybe have gotten a few seconds of attention on the local news tonight—a student protest about an obscure staff policy isn't that interesting. But the suggestion of the school board instituting an unnecessary and possibly discriminatory policy has earmarks of corruption all over it, and that's going to attract more attention. Maybe more investigation."

She's… right. Wow. I can't believe I never thought of that.

"I feel a little bit sorry for the board," I admit, surprising myself. "Most of them weren't that bad."

"Don't feel sorry for them," Darryn says, and we turn to see him in the doorway. "So this is where you're hiding. Can you see…?" He looks out the window. "Oh, this is a great view."

"We just watched you being interviewed," Jaiden says.

"I figured, based on what you were saying." He cocks an eyebrow at me. "Don't worry about the board. A spotlight right now may be exactly what they need."

A lot has happened to me this week, and I'm blaming all of that for the fact that my brain hasn't been doing its best work. It's not exactly surprising that it's taken me until right this second to think about my meeting with Darryn on Monday—and the confrontation that came after.

"Oh my god, the board did this on purpose," I breathe.

Jaiden and Lindy look a mixture of concerned and confused, because obviously the board decision wasn't an accident, but Darryn grins.

"I don't know that it was on purpose, exactly," he

says. "But the more level-headed members were fairly certain that a policy like this wouldn't stand up to any pressure."

"Wait." Jaiden's eyes widen. "They agreed to a policy they knew they'd need to revoke?"

It's all coming together in my head. "The sticks. They agreed to placate the sticks." I realize how weird that sounds. "Uh—"

But Darryn's shaking his head and chuckling. "I can't say for sure, but that's where I'd put my money. I'd also say that the attention this will bring down on the board might result in some resignations." He shrugs. "Who knows?" As he backs toward the door, he says, "I suggest you lie low over the weekend, though, if you don't want to talk to the press. Oh, and just so you know, the chairman advised me earlier today that they've received a letter from the union and have heard about a petition that's being circulated around town, which I'm sure will be forwarded to them soon also. If you were planning to send a letter of protest or anything, it probably wouldn't hurt." He disappears into the hallway, leaving me with my jaw dropped.

"Did you talk to a lawyer?" Jaiden asks.

I close my mouth and nod. "They actually sent me a letter this morning to forward to the board. I haven't yet, because…" I don't know why. I want to say it's been a busy day, but how long does it take to forward an email?

Could it be that I was hoping someone else would fix this for me? That the student protest, the petition, the union, and my colleagues' complaints would force the board to reverse their decision without me having to take any action?

I hate that the answer I'm hiding from is almost

certainly "yes." That's not the person I try to be. That's not the person I want to be. And worse, if it's true, then was Dom really so far out of line? Oh, not with the broken promise or with his assumption that I'd leave Joyville—he crossed lines there—but with wanting to step in and take care of this for me. To look after me. If he'd done things just a little bit differently, would I have gladly let him fix this for me?

Something I need to think about.

In the meantime…

"I guess I should go forward it now." I glance out the window again. The press is leaving, and the rally will probably break up soon, since the end of the school day is in a few minutes and some of the students need to take the bus home.

It's time for me to take my own action.

SEVENTEEN

Dom

L ate Friday afternoon, Layla walks into my office without knocking. "Have you seen?" she demands, coming over to my desk.

"Seen what?" If she's talking about the marketing report, I'm looking at it right now. Elise is going to have a lot of explaining to do next week.

Layla rolls her eyes and huffs, then turns my laptop toward her and taps at the keyboard. "There." She turns it back. It's a local news site, and the headline is—

Oh, fuck! Cara's protest rally was today. I meant to check in with her about it. A glance at the clock shows it's definitely over now. Should I call or wait until I get home?

The video on the screen starts to play, capturing my attention. It's been edited, but Jamie and Cara still both sound great—clear, sensible, mature. Nobody could suggest that this is just an excuse to get out of school or cause trouble, not for them, anyway. A grin spreads across my face.

"Your daughter is one in a million," Layla tells me fondly, and I glance up to see her grinning too.

"I've always thought so." I scan the crowd in the background of the video. It's not likely Oliver would be there, but I can't help looking anyway. I haven't heard from him at all this week, although Cara says she spoke to him and that he seems okay, under the circumstances.

And then the school principal starts to speak, and my attention snaps back to the foreground of the video. "Well, well," I murmur as his subtext makes it very clear that he thinks the board has acted wrongly. "Oliver said the principal supported him, but this is a lot further than I thought he'd go."

"Interesting, isn't it?" Layla says smugly. "I knew I liked this guy. My bet is that things will go back to normal before the end of next week."

"You don't think the board will wait to make a decision until the next meeting?" I'm only half paying attention to our conversation, my focus still on the screen.

"Nah," she declares. "There's a lot of bad feelings about this in town. A lot of people with kids have connections to teachers at that school—family, friends, neighbors. Nobody wants to see their kid's teacher punished because they happen to live across the street from each other. This new policy wasn't really clear on what a 'personal connection' is. I've spoken to Oliver on the phone a few times because I work for you—does that mean my kids have a personal connection to him? Where's the line?" She shakes her head. "The community is unhappy, and Sascha Weston is on the warpath. Between that, what those kids have done," she nods toward my laptop, "and any official complaints from the teachers and union, the board is going to be doing a backflip as soon as they can manage it."

I hope she's right.

There's a perfunctory knock on my open door, and Luke walks in without waiting for me to look up. "Hey, have you— Oh, good, you're watching it." He joins Layla in leaning over my desk. "Just letting you know, there's a group of parents organizing a letter to the board. They asked me to tell you 'unofficially' that you're not going to be asked to sign it because of your relationship with Oliver." His gaze is steady on me, and I nod. It's been hard to pretend everything between me and Oliver is okay, and having some people know the truth makes it a little easier.

The video comes to an end, and Luke and Layla straighten.

"Layla thinks this will all be over next week," I tell Luke, who considers it.

"You might be right. There's a lot of pressure being brought to bear."

"See?" Layla tells me, cocking her hip and planting a hand on it. "You should listen to me more often." On that note, she heads for the door. "I'm leaving half an hour early today, so if you need anything before I go, you've got ten minutes to let me know."

"Just go now. I'm set, and I won't be staying late tonight."

"I knew I did the right thing taking this job." She waves and saunters out. Luke waits a moment, then lowers his voice so she won't hear.

"How are you?"

I shrug. "Getting by. Keeping busy and distracted."

He nods. "Good. Mila called before—the kids who

organized the rally are going out for pizza, so Cara's probably not going to be home tonight. Want to come to our place for dinner?"

I hesitate, and he adds, "Derek's coming too. He actually invited himself."

Oh—that's right. It's Friday, so Trav will be working, and so will Jason. Dimi too, but mostly because he's a control freak rather than because there's an actual need for him to be there.

"Sure," I agree. "Just let me make sure—"

As if on cue, my phone chimes with a text, and sure enough, it's Cara telling me she won't be home for dinner.

"That's incredible timing," I say dryly, and Luke laughs.

"Kids are really good at that kind of timing. So just come around when you're done here, yeah?"

"Want me to bring anything?"

He backs toward the door, shaking his head. "Nah, we're set. I've already let Jas know we'll have extra people. She said something about meatloaf and cobbler."

My mouth starts to water. "I might have to offer her a job working for me."

He stops dead four feet from the door and glares. "You're uninvited to dinner."

Laughing, I wave him off, and the satisfied smirk on his face as he leaves makes me think he mostly came to check on me.

I'm nearly ready to pack it in for the week when my phone trills with the tone I assigned for my boss, the CEO of Joy Incorporated, Malcolm Joy. That's not uncommon, but since we have our regular monthly status meeting scheduled for Monday, it's a bit concerning. What could have happened that can't wait unt—

I groan.

Fucking gossip. Fucking online news.

Sucking in a deep breath, I answer. "Hey, Mal."

"I've got Seth here with me, so don't say anything horrible about him," Malcolm jokes, and the vise around my chest loosens a little. Whatever this is about, it's unlikely they're going to fire me with an opening like that.

"Hi, Seth," I say to Joy Inc's CFO—and Malcolm's cousin.

"Hi, Dom. Does that mean you both say horrible things about me when I'm not around?" he asks, a faint thread of laughter in his voice.

"Absolutely. I call Mal twice a week to say nasty things about you. I thought you knew."

"I must have missed that memo. Listen, we know it's late there, but—"

"Why didn't you tell us your boyfriend was being discriminated against?" Malcolm demands.

Seth groans.

I take a moment to decide what to say. There are a few reasons, starting with the fact that officially, it's not overtly discrimination, but one has to be tactful when talking to the boss, and I don't think "It's none of your business" is the right way to go.

"I didn't think it was relevant to the company" is what I finally settle on.

I'm not sure which one of them snorts—possibly both, it's hard to tell over the phone—but I have a sneaking suspicion I'm finally going to be subjected to the busybody antics Luke insists they inflicted on him.

"Dom," Seth says patiently, "you're running a huge branch of our business. Pretty much everything about you is relevant to the company."

He's not exactly wrong, but I still open my mouth to say something about Oliver's right to privacy. Malcolm beats me to it.

"From what we've heard and what we've just seen, your position is the basis for what's happening right now. If you weren't the director of Joy Universe, it's unlikely that this would have occurred. Correct?"

I frown. "What have you seen?" The clip I just watched had minimal information, was mostly just an overview of the rally and the publicly stated reasons for it. It sounds like they've watched something a lot more detailed... and possibly investigative.

"I'll send you a link," Seth promises. "But was what Mal said right?"

"I can't say for certain, but it's my belief. Wait, what have you *heard*?" I really thought that, despite Luke's darkly ominous warnings, news of my love life hadn't traveled to head office in LA. Neither Malcolm nor Seth has said anything to me about it over the past few months. They've asked about Cara and how she'd settled in, what her plans are after she graduates—the usual casual chitchat. I ask them about their grandkids. But maybe I was kidding myself?

"Don't freak out," Malcolm says, and he sounds exactly like Cara does when she's rolling her eyes at me, which is a disconcerting thought. "We hear things here. We made a little bit of money in the pool, but not as much as we hoped."

"You're a sneaky bastard, Dom," Seth grumbles. "I

was *certain* things wouldn't progress between you two until Cara had graduated."

I have no idea what I'm supposed to say to that.

Wait, yes, I do.

"Serves you right for betting on my life."

There's a mix of snorting and chuckling that sounds rather disturbing.

"Anyway," Mal declares, "we're sending a letter to the town council and the school board, reminding them that we expect any and all policies enacted by them to be completely legal and nondiscriminatory."

I wince. "I've been trying to keep JU out of it," I confess. "I don't want it to look like I'm using my influence on behalf of my boyfriend." I'm relieved and proud that I manage that word without a hitch in my voice. "And Oliver has already said he doesn't want me involved."

"He's right," Seth agrees. "Which is why the letter is coming from us."

"Do you even have an official leg to stand on?" The town may give the director of JU, and by extension Joy Inc, nominal positions on various boards, but legally I don't think we have any real say.

"No, but since we don't interfere very often and we do fund a lot of grants and public works, the town council tends to listen when we make suggestions. And from what we've seen so far, they're already feeling a lot of pressure over this. Even if the board isn't inclined to change their minds—although I think they are—the council will lean hard very soon. There are some strict antidiscrimination ordinances in place in Joyville, and this stomps all over them."

I can't argue with that. "I'll leave it in your hands, then."

"Excellent. If anyone asks, you were aware that we'd decided to send the letter but chose to remove yourself from any discussions about it because of your personal interest."

"Fine by me. I'll refer any questions back to head office."

"Then that's done," Malcolm declares. "Now, how are you coping with this shit?"

There's a moment of pure panic before I realize he's still talking about the school board drama, not about me and Oliver. "It's been a week," I say noncommittally.

"I'll bet it has," Seth commiserates. "You seem to have a lot of support there, though."

"Okay, who the hell have you been talking to?" I demand exasperatedly. "Do you have spies around here? Am I going to have to ferret them out?"

"We'll never reveal our secrets," Mal says dramatically.

"It's Luke, isn't it?" His job is split between the two offices, so he's in contact with his team members in LA almost daily. Plus he has a direct line to Malcolm and Seth. It wouldn't surprise me at all if a few idle comments on his part have kicked up a storm of gossip at head office.

"Why would you think it's Luke?" Seth says with the worst fake surprise ever.

I snort. "Please."

"Anyway, we'll let you go," Mal cuts in. "Look after yourself, and if there's anything we can do to support you or Oliver, just say the word. This is going to get better soon."

"Thank you." I'm genuinely touched by the offer, even if my feelings are bittersweet.

"And if you could announce plans to get married between twelve and fifteen months from now, that would be appreciated. That's what Mal and I got in the pool," Seth adds.

"What—" But I'm speaking to the dial tone.

Jesus fucking Christ. People are betting on when we'll get married?

I need a drink.

I HEAD STRAIGHT to Luke and Grant's place, not bothering to go home and change or drop off my laptop. Luke opens the door for me, smiling, and I jab a finger at him.

"You're an asshole."

His smile disappears, and he blinks. "I am? What did I do?"

I push past him into the house, glancing around quickly to make sure neither of his kids are within earshot. "Been talking to Seth and Malcolm lately?" I hiss, and he winces.

"Oh." He closes the front door. "In my defense, they seemed to know an awful lot without my help. I think they might have spies in the office." The joke falls flat, even though it echoes what I said not that long ago.

"There's a betting pool on when Oliver and I are going to announce our engagement!" My whisper is a lot louder and sharper than I intended, and I look around again. Luke notices.

"Oh, don't worry. The kids aren't here. Mila's with

Cara, remember, and Jordan's at a birthday sleepover. It's just me and Grant and Derek."

All of whom know my secrets. And are apparently betting on them.

Why did I want friends, again?

"Got beer?" I ask. I won't drink much with driving and Cara coming home later, but a beer to take the edge off this week would be really good.

He jerks his head toward the kitchen. "Come on."

I follow him down the hall to where the inviting smells seem to be coming from. Grant's at the counter, mashing potatoes, and Derek's setting the table. Jas, one of the twins who look after Luke's house and kids, is just pulling a dish out of the oven and setting it on the stovetop.

"Okay, I'm off. You all can dish up for yourselves." She glances over her shoulder toward us and smiles. "Hi, Dom." Her eyes move past me, as if she's expecting to see someone else, and she frowns for a second before turning back to Grant. "You remember the instructions for the cobbler?"

"Yes, Jas. I promise I won't fuck it up."

"And even if he does, it'll still be good," Luke chimes in. "Go home. We'll see you next week." There's a flurry of goodbyes, and then she's gone and Luke is passing me a beer while Grant serves up the meatloaf, potatoes, and green beans.

It's not until the first forkful is in my mouth that I realize Jas was looking for Oliver before. Probably wondering why he wasn't here. The food instantly turns to ashes in my mouth, which is a travesty, since it tasted amazing up until now.

I force myself to swallow and then wash it down with a mouthful of beer. "I hate you all," I announce.

"Why?" Derek asks plaintively. He's used to being universally liked, even by people who hate him.

"Bets. On. My. Nonexistent. *Engagement.*"

Grant flinches.

"Ouch," Derek says. "Yeah. You weren't supposed to find out."

I grab my beer bottle in a strangling grip.

"What I mean is," he hurries on, "we can't exactly put a stop to that bet without telling people…" He trails off at the look I give him.

"There's no known way to stop the betting," Grant says. "I'm sorry, but it's true. Someone always starts something on the sly. I really wish you hadn't heard about this one, though."

Sighing, I let go of the bottle and grab my fork again. "I know. I just…"

"You feel like crap right now and finding out about this was a kick in the teeth," Luke finishes.

I nod and shovel meatloaf into my mouth. It doesn't taste as good as before, but it's better than ashes, so I guess I'm feeling better?

"What did Malcolm and Seth have to say, anyway?" he asks curiously. "Did they just call to lean on you about your engagement announcement?"

I shake my head, chewing, then swallow. "No, they wanted to let me know they're sending a letter to the school board that I'm supposed to know about but have recused myself from. And they asked why I hadn't told them what was going on."

Derek laughs. "Yeah, because you were going to run

to your bosses and tell them your boyfriend's boss was being mean to him."

I point my fork at him. "Right? And Oliver and I decided right from the beginning to keep JU out of our relationship. But they said it was pretty clear that he's being punished because I'm the director, and I can't really argue with that."

There're nods all around the table.

"So what's this letter going to say?" Luke asks, and I shrug.

"They said it would be a reminder to act in a legal and nondiscriminatory matter."

"Low-pressure pressure," Derek says sagely. "They can't really do anything, but the school board had better remember who paid for the renovation to the art facilities a few years back. And I heard the board wants a new sports complex and is hoping JU will help fund it."

"How did you hear that?" I demand, and he smirks.

"Dimi, of course. He's not my assistant anymore, but I still keep the information pathways open."

There's really no good response to that.

"There's pressure from all over," I conclude. "It's likely that the board will cave. Especially if someone decides to raise a legal challenge." I take another mouthful. The fact is, this situation with the school board will resolve itself, but it's not going to change how I've managed to fuck up my life.

EIGHTEEN

Oliver

_____

One Month Later

I can't deny the satisfaction I feel at the end of a Friday afternoon. No matter how the week has been, the moment the last bell of the day rings and the students make their escape, I feel immensely satisfied with a job well done.

However, lately it's been a bittersweet feeling. Sure, I've done a great job in the classroom and for the school in general, especially now that I'm once again head of the English department, but it's hard to avoid—or be happy about—the knowledge that I'm going home to an empty house and endless hours of loneliness that nothing seems to fill.

I used to live alone and love it. I never needed the sound of another person in the house to make me happy. I had my own space, a social life with friends, books and music, and the never-ending entertainment of the internet and streaming services. I still have all those things, and I still enjoy them, but there's a place in me that's hollow, no matter what I do.

It's stupid, because even when I was with Dom, even when we were hanging out together in the evening, it's not like we were constantly talking. Sometimes I'd read or watch TV and he'd work, or I'd be grading assignments while he did his thing. So the loneliness is more about missing *him* than anything else.

Not even *Poldark* makes me feel better.

Which is why I spent several hours last Sunday trying to approach this in a logical manner. Don't laugh —I let my geek have free rein. The result? I decided there are three possible options.

First: Continue like I am. It's only been a month since Dom and I broke up. Maybe things will get better. They have to eventually, right? And it would probably help if people knew we'd actually broken up. For some reason I don't fully understand—*lie*—it's still a secret from everyone but our closest friends. I'm kind of shocked we've managed that, given the way gossip goes in this town. So option one is to put the relationship behind me and find a way to move on.

Second: Attempt to fill the loneliness with random hookups until my leftover feelings for Dom are quite literally fucked out of me. Although this plan looks like a lot of fun on the surface, the idea of being with a stranger turns me off. That surprised me at first, since I had my share of one-nighters when I was younger, but I guess I've changed.

Third: Talk to Dom and see if maybe we can salvage something between us.

There are pros and cons to each option, things that excite me and/or scare me. In the end, I decided to give myself the workweek to think about it, no pressure to decide—just think.

Option one is the easiest. It would mean doing nothing. But on the flip side, nothing would change, and I'd be stuck with this horrible emptiness.

Option two holds the least appeal. I really don't want to pick up a stranger for sex. And really, will that make me any less lonely once the sex is done?

Option three... well, option three is the scariest, and yet the one I yearn toward the most. Option three has the power to stomp the last few working pieces of my heart to dust. It might also be the thing that fixes everything and gives me back my life.

I guess what it comes down to is how I feel now. When I told Dom to get out, I was so angry and hurt. I was shattered. I felt like my trust had been betrayed. I felt like he didn't *see* me. To a certain extent, that hasn't changed. I don't feel that I was wrong to react as I did. However... he's apologized and admitted he was in the wrong. He's expressed the wish to apologize again. And he's respected my wishes and complied with my requests since then. People make mistakes, right? And it wasn't exactly a normal situation. I was under a lot of pressure, and he acted out of a desire to protect me. Sure, he made the wrong decision, but he knows it. And, with the benefit of a lot of soul searching, I can say that if we'd been different people, if he wasn't the director and it hadn't been his kid tangled up in everything, I probably would have welcomed having him attempt to take care of me. I like that he wants to look after things like that, that he can be a little dominant.

We were both incredibly stressed that night. If things had gone just a tiny bit differently, or if the phone had rung and interrupted our fight, chances are we would have avoided those last devastating moments, slept apart, cooled off, and discussed it again the next day. He would have accepted that there was no way I'd leave the school and admitted it was his anger talking. I would have understood why he'd chosen to break his promise and accepted his apology—and apologized for not letting him share my burden the way I really wanted him to. I'd been so caught up in not wanting people to treat me differently because I was dating the director that I failed to see I was letting it influence our relationship, and I never even really talked to him about my problems.

So the question now is: Do I trust that Dom's actions were one-off, the result of a highly stressful situation, and that he'd go out of his way to avoid ever doing that again? Can I give him another chance?

More to the point, does he want another chance? It's been a month. The only communication we've had was those texts the morning after that night. Maybe he's put me behind him and is moving on with life. Maybe he's maintained the ruse of us being together still because he doesn't want people gossiping that he's interested in every second person he runs into on the street.

Or worst of all... maybe he's using our "relationship" as a shield to hide the fact that he's seeing someone else, to protect them from Joyville's gossip circuit.

I honestly don't know. The only way to find out is to talk to Dom, lay my cards out on the table.

I groan and bang my head against my desk.

"Problem?"

I turn my head to glare at Jaiden without bothering

to lift it. I made the mistake early this week of telling him about my options, and since then he's taken every opportunity to put his two cents in. He's my best friend, and I love him, but sometimes I want to strangle him.

He sighs, steps into my classroom, and closes the door. Not that there are that many people still around to overhear us.

"Still trying to decide?"

Groaning again, I straighten. "Not really. I know what I need to do. The problem is, I'm terrified of what might happen." I wait for him to tell me I'm being dramatic, but he just leans against my desk with a thoughtful expression.

Panic spikes.

"Seriously? This is where you're supposed to lecture me about facing my fears."

He nods. "Yeah, but would you listen? I've been saying stuff like that all week, and it hasn't made any difference."

I hate that he's right.

"However," he adds, and I can't help the tiny snort that erupts from me. "I think it might help if you think about everything that's happened this month."

Say what?

He must see my confusion, because he continues without me having to ask him to.

"The board took the path of least resistance and screwed you over because a judgmental old woman happened to have some influence with some of the most bullheaded and persistent members. Most of them knew their decision wouldn't stand, but that's still no excuse for fucking with your life. The drama led to you and Dom breaking up."

"Thanks for the recap." Is this supposed to be helping?

"Then the entire town rallied to defend your rights," he goes on, and I'm about to tell him not to exaggerate, but... he's right.

Wow.

The whole town supported me. I mean, they were also defending the rights of *all* the teachers in town, but it was only me being affected in this instance.

"Your students, and many who've never been your students but respect you all the same, turned out to show the board they were wrong. Your colleagues did the same. The board was forced to rescind their idiotic policy less than two weeks after implementing it. You got reinstated to your job with an official apology from the board. None of that makes up for being screwed over, but I'd say it shows you just how valued you are."

There's a warm feeling in my chest. Yes, it does make me feel valued. I can't deny that things have been different lately. People were always nice to me, but there's been a more overt effort to include me. They're going out of their way to make up for me having been put through the wringer. It's... nice.

Even if my poor broken heart can't fully appreciate it.

And just like that, I get what Jaiden's trying to tell me. If I can't feel welcome and appreciated and content with most of the town giving me the metaphorical equivalent of a big hug, then nothing can make it happen. I need to act. Maybe things won't go the way I want them to; maybe Dom will crush the remnants of my heart. But I'll know. I'll be able to let go, to recover, and to move on, no matter how hard it is. I won't be trapped in this painful stasis.

I guess that means I've made up my mind.

"Let's get out of here," I say, my throat dry. How am I going to do this?

Ugh. I thought choosing an option was the hard part, but now that I know what I'm going to do, there's a whole slew of other choices I need to make.

And then I actually have to carry them out.

I've had my phone in my hand for an hour.

Officially, I'm watching TV. I've had dinner, gotten some grading out of the way so I won't have to do it this weekend, and I'm all comfy-cozy on my couch.

The text has been written. It took me six attempts before I was happy with the wording—and that was after I spent twenty minutes wondering if I should call instead. But it's still waiting to be sent.

Every minute, my screen goes dark and I have to wake it up again. All I have to do is hit Send and I can put my phone down. Although that probably won't happen, because I'll be agonizing over whether he's seen it and when he'll text back—*if* he texts back.

Should I wait until morning? Will I be able to sleep tonight if he doesn't reply right away? Or what if he says he's not interested in meeting up? Or, even if he does agree to meet up, will I be able to sleep knowing that we're going to meet?

This is ridiculous. I'm not going to sleep no matter what I do.

I hit Send.

Never has that whooshing sound filled me with such dread. I instantly want to turn back time and not send that message… but at the same time, I feel a lot calmer.

Oliver: Hi Dom. Can we meet? I'd like us to talk.

It takes literally seconds before "Delivered" changes to "Read," and then there are three dancing dots on the screen. He's replying.

Dom: Yes. Definitely. Whenever you want. Now?

Oh. I'd actually been thinking tomorrow, over coffee maybe, but now would mean not having to toss and turn all night while my brain manufactures scenarios of how it can all go wrong.

Although… I look down at myself. I'm really not dressed for—

My phone whooshes again, and I look down at the new message he sent.

Dom: I could come over, if you don't want to go out. Or you could come here. Cara's out.

Another whoosh.

Dom: Or tomorrow is fine. Anytime. Just say when.

My nerves start to settle, and a tiny smile tugs at my lips—my first real smile in weeks. It sounds like he's as nervous about this as I am, and he probably wouldn't be if he'd moved on… right?

Oliver: Now would be good, if you don't mind coming over?

I've barely hit Send before he replies.

Dom: On my way.

I put the phone down and take a deep breath… and then panic crashes in. I leap to my feet and race into the bedroom to change out of my old, worn sweats and into… what do you wear when your ex who you probably want to get back with comes over to talk?

In the end, I settle on newer sweatpants and a

brand-new Henley. It's a Friday night at home, and Dom knows me. Anything else would have looked like I was trying too hard and made us both uncomfortable. I do take time to brush my hair and make sure my beard is neat, though. And I do a quick whizz around the house and check for… I actually have no idea what I'm checking for. Anything that's out of place, I guess.

I'm standing in front of the couch, doing absolutely nothing, just standing, when the doorbell rings, and it still feels like I'm not ready. I'm getting disgusted with myself now—even when I was a dramatic, hormonal teenager, I didn't act like this.

I wish I could say that when I open the door to Dom, everything fell into place. That there was a movie moment—that our eyes met and all our problems became inconsequential. That we fell into each other's arms and kissed and the camera faded to show The End. There'd also be a suitably romantic backing track, something that swells with passion and intensity but still leaves you feeling warm inside.

That doesn't happen.

Instead, I stand there like a lump, blocking him from entering while we stare at each other and the cool night air whisks into my house. It's actually the cold that wakes me up—I shiver, and that makes my brain kick into gear.

I step aside. "Hey. Uh. Thanks for coming. Come in." That's not too bad, right? Not exactly a prize-worthy speech, but complete sentences that make sense are always a good thing.

He comes in. I close the door. We both stand awkwardly in the entryway.

"Um. Living room?" I may be losing that complete-sentences ability I was so proud of a minute ago.

His mouth moves in what could probably be called a smile if his whole face wasn't so tense, and he says, "Sure. Thanks."

So we go into the living room. The TV is still playing, even though I can't for the life of me remember it being on when the doorbell rang—which tells you how far in my head I was—and I look around for a second before just deciding to sit on the couch. Dom sits at the other end. Part of me wishes he'd opted for the armchair, but this is better, and he's not so close that I feel crowded.

He watches me warily. "I was really glad to get your message," he says quietly. "I want to apologize again for —for that night. For the things I said. For breaking my promise."

I take a deep breath. "Thank you. I-It was a difficult night for both of us. I think things got out of hand." I look at my hands, folded in my lap. "I wish you hadn't broken your promise, but I get why you did."

"I wish I hadn't. And I never will again, if you… I mean, if we… I wouldn't break a promise to you again. I should have trusted that you'd tell me if you needed more from me. Not respecting you in that way was the stupidest thing I've ever done. And then I made it worse by telling you to quit and teach at a college." He shakes his head, lips twisted with disgust. "That was so stupid. You wouldn't be happy there. If I hadn't been so angry, I would never have even said it."

I'd already thought that, but hearing him say it is balm to a wound deep inside. It reinforces my resolve that this is what I want.

"I think that if we'd had time to cool off before too much was said, it would have been our first big fight instead of the fight that broke us up."

He nods. "We were angry about other things and took that out on each other. Not that I didn't do the wrong thing, but—"

I hold up a hand. "I get it. You've apologized now, and I've accepted it. We can move on from that. And I agree, we were both stressed and pissed off and made convenient targets for each other. I…" I look away for a second before focusing on him again. His blue eyes are so hopeful. "I was so caught up in not wanting to take advantage of your position as the director that I ignored the fact you were also my boyfriend and I was allowed to lean on you for support. That frustrated me, although I didn't realize it at the time."

A tentative smile crosses his face, and I smile back. We sit there for a minute in slightly awkward silence.

"Uh, so…" He inhales deeply. "Do you… Can we… I don't want to pressure…"

"Dom?"

He stops and waits, and even though I'm completely sure that this is what we both want, there are still butterflies in my stomach.

"Can we get back together?"

He breaks out in a grin and lunges forward. I meet him halfway, and nothing has ever felt as good as being back in his arms, his mouth on mine. In moments we're sprawled on my comfy old couch, tangled together, rubbing against each other as we kiss. Oh my god, I missed this so much. Our clothing melts away between kisses, but I drag him up before things can go further. We have no lube here, and I want him in me so bad.

"Bedroom," I say when he pouts, and he immediately brightens. We race each other down the hall, bursting into the room laughing and diving for the bed. It's silly and immature, but I love that I can be silly and immature with him.

He peppers my face with kisses, muttering about how he missed my eyes and my nose and my beard, then works his way south, telling me how beautiful my clavicle is. I snort and pull his mouth back to mine.

"I—was—busy," he says between kisses. "I have—to lavish—your body—with affection." He takes hold of my cock and squeezes lightly, leaving no room to mistake what he means.

"Not this time," I order. "I want to come with you in me."

He shudders, probably at the image those words conjure, and nods. "Your wish is my command."

Snickering, I lean across to the nightstand and open the drawer for the lube. My gaze lands on a couple of loose condoms that have been in there for far too long—and I still. Dom and I got tested and stopped using condoms months ago, but...

"What's wrong?" He leans up behind me and kisses my shoulder.

"I—" I shake my head to clear it, then turn to look at him. "Do we, uh, do we need a condom?" My stomach is in knots waiting for the answer. I haven't even been able to seriously consider sleeping with someone else, and I don't think he has either, but part of me is still terrified that *maybe*...

He shifts to a sitting position and pulls me around so we're facing each other properly. "I haven't been with anyone but you since last July," he says bluntly, and I feel weak with relief.

"I haven't been with anyone else either," I mumble, and a smile breaks across his face.

"Then all we need is this." He leans over to grab the lube and firmly shuts the drawer on the condoms.

It only takes moments for us to get back in the mood. It's been too long since we were together, and neither of us wants to spend too much time on foreplay. We'll have time for that later—forever—but now, we just need to be connected again. I rush him through stretching me and then finally, *finally*, he's pushing in, the burn a lovely reminder that he's mine, he's in me, we're together.

When he bottoms out, he kisses me, our tongues dueling, and we don't break the kiss except to breathe and murmur words of encouragement as he thrusts, in and out, a steady rhythm that hits me just right, until it becomes unsteady as we soar higher and higher and then he works a hand between us and grips my dick, stroking in time with his thrusts.

I explode.

The pieces that used to be me settle as he shouts, his body going taut in my arms.

Where he belongs.

Epilogue

DOM

My heart is being torn in two.

As I watch my baby girl cross the stage and accept her high school diploma, I force a smile. I can't believe she's graduating. I can't believe that in just a few months, she'll be off to college. Where the hell did the years go?

But at the same time, I am so, *so* proud of her.

Beside me, Tia sighs and whispers, "Look how amazing she is. How did we make that?" She arranged a special trip so she could be here for today. It looks like her secondment is going to be extended and she'll be in Japan for at least a year longer than originally planned. She asked Cara which she'd prefer, that Tia be here for her graduation or to help her move into her dorm when college starts, and Cara voted for graduation. Personally, I get the feeling Tia's going to try to be here for both, but she hasn't said it outright.

"If she didn't look like you, I'd think we'd taken the wrong baby home from the hospital," I murmur back. Neither of us believe that, of course. Cara's a lot like both of us: driven and focused. But still… she outshines us both.

And she's all grown up.

Cara leaves the stage, and Tia turns to me. "We have to stay until the end, don't we?"

"Yes. It would be disrespectful if we didn't. And Cara and Oliver both threatened me with death if we tried to sneak out early." Not that either of us would, even if we did want to.

And we do.

Scanning the crowd, Tia asks, "Where is your sexy professor, anyway?" She's been calling him that since Cara first sent her a picture, right after Christmas, and even though Oliver pointed out he's not a professor and —in his words—not sexy, he hasn't asked her to stop. In fact, the way he blushes when she says it led to a *very* fun role-playing experience in his bedroom one night.

Okay, maybe more than just one night.

"He's over there with the rest of the faculty." I point to the rows of chairs to the side of the stage. I really missed him when it was Cara's turn to receive her diploma—it would've been nice to hold his hand. I really never thought this would hit me so hard.

The ceremony goes on for what seems like forever, but finally comes to an end. Cara comes to find us, and Tia squeezes her until she yelps, then wipes away a tear.

Cara and I stare. Tia is not a crier.

"Shut up," she says. "I'm allowed to be emotional at my only child's high school graduation."

"Of course you are, Mom," Cara agrees. "But that doesn't mean we're not surprised." She kisses her mom on the cheek. "I'm so glad you're here."

Tia breathes in deep through her nose, like she's

trying to control an emotional reaction, and Cara and I laugh.

I sling an arm around my grown-up daughter's shoulders and press a kiss to the side of her head. "Congratulations, sweetheart. I'm so proud of you."

She leans into my side. "Thanks, Dad. Are we ready to go? Where's Oliver?"

Gesturing to where he's approaching but has been waylaid by another student, I say, "Yep, but it looks like it'll be a minute." We asked Cara what she wanted to do to celebrate her graduation, if she wanted to go out or even go away for a few days, and she asked for a barbecue with our friends. Oliver offered his house, since obviously the condo doesn't have a yard.

On the topic of the condo, my lease expires in a few months, and I won't be renewing it. Oliver and I have decided there's no point in us playing musical houses any longer. It's rare that we spend a night apart anymore, and with Cara leaving right around that time, we figured it worked out best. There's room for her when she's home on break, and the house will be more comfortable than the condo, even as nice as it is. I'm looking forward to the move.

Finally, Oliver detaches himself from the last student and makes his way over.

"Congratulations, Cara," he says, holding out his hand. "I can't wait to see you let loose on the world."

She laughs and shakes his hand, then surprises us all by hugging him. "Thanks, Oliver. I can't either!"

SITTING BACK with a full belly and a beer in hand, I glance around the yard and can't help but smile. It's so weird to think that only a little over nine months ago, I hadn't met most of these people. Luke and Grant were both on the hiring panel that interviewed me, and I knew if I got the job, they'd be working for me, but I never thought they'd end up being my friends. My focus was on whether they'd be good to work with. Now, even though I work with them—and most of the others—I think of them first as friends. That's a little dangerous, seeing as I'm their boss, but I'm also secure in the knowledge that I can trust them not to take advantage of it.

Across the table, Dimi and Derek are arguing over something trivial while Trav rolls his eyes and Jason eggs them on. Nearby, Sascha Weston and her husband—whose name I shockingly didn't know until he was introduced to me today—are talking to Oliver and Tia about Sascha's plan to apply for the school board.

Oh, did I forget to mention? After the board caved to pressure and rescinded the new policy, the two members who'd pushed for it in the first place resigned in protest. Nobody was sorry to see them go. In fact, if gossip can be believed—which in this town, it usually can—their resignations saved the rest of the board from having to find a way to oust them. And Edith Hamilton, who according to Oliver was the root of all the trouble, has officially retired as of the last day of school. So we've all got high hopes for the next school year, even if for me those hopes are as a faculty significant other rather than a parent.

Because I'll no longer be the parent of a high schooler.

The kids—Cara, Mila, Jordan, and some of Cara's friends who aren't celebrating with their own families until later—have gathered at the far end of the yard and look like they're having a great time. There's lots of grins and laughter.

I'm smiling kind of wistfully in their direction when Oliver comes up beside me, slips an arm around my waist, and leans in. I lean right back, loving the comfort of having him pressed against me.

"She's here a few months more," he says quietly, following my gaze.

"Yeah, I know. I'm not even sad, really. I want her to live her best life and experience… well, not everything. But most things." I turn my head and kiss his cheek, savoring the sensation of his beard under my lips. "I was just thinking how much has changed in a year. I'm so glad we're here. Glad for the people in my life. You, especially."

He smiles and rests his head against mine. We stand there, wrapped up in each other, and I love him so much that it causes an ache deep down inside.

Realization is like a slap. I blink. It can't be true… can it?

Except it is.

Months together, a breakup, making up… and neither of us have said those three words that often get tossed around so casually.

I feel it. I've felt it since before we broke up. I know he does too. I don't need him to tell me to know—it's in his every action. In the quiet times we spend together. In the hot, sweaty confines of our bed. Sometimes, words aren't necessary.

But that doesn't mean they're not a nice bonus.

Putting my lips to his ear, I whisper, "I love you."

A smile breaks over his face. He meets my gaze, and sure enough, it's all there: everything I don't need words to know. Leaning forward, he kisses me, the merest brush of his lips against mine.

And whispers, "Love you."

Hi from Louisa!

Hey folks! Thanks so much for reading *Take Us There*. I hope you enjoyed this final installment in the Joy Universe series!

If you missed out on the rest of the series, Derek and Trav's book, *I've Got This*, Dimi and Jason's book, *Follow My Lead*, and Luke and Grant's book, *In Your Hands*, are available now for sale and in Kindle Unlimited. I also have a sneaky little free novella set in JU—you can download it now by subscribing to my newsletter at https://claims.prolificwords.com/free/Rpl-OchBm. You can unsubscribe anytime—or stick around for regular freebies and bonus content.

Please take a moment if you're so inclined to leave a review for *Follow My Lead*. Reviews can make a huge difference to a book's visibility. And to find out more about me and my books, check out my website or visit my author group, Seymour Books with Masterful Men.

Hugs! Louisa xx

Also by Louisa Masters

Hidden Species

Demons Do It Better

One Bite With A Vampire (coming soon)

Met His Match

Charming Him

Offside Rules

Between the Covers (M/F)

Joy Universe

I've Got This

Follow My Lead

In Your Hands

Novellas

Fake It 'Til You Make It (permafree)

Out of the Office

After the Blaze

About the Author

Louisa Masters started reading romance much earlier than her mother thought she should. While other teenagers were sneaking out of the house, Louisa was sneaking romance novels in and working out how to read them without being discovered. As an adult, she feeds her addiction in every spare second. She spent years trying to build a "sensible" career, working in bookstores, recruitment, resource management, administration, and as a travel agent, before finally conceding defeat and devoting herself to the world of romance novels.

Louisa has a long list of places first discovered in books that she wants to visit, and every so often she overcomes her loathing of jet lag and takes a trip that charges her imagination. She lives in Melbourne, Australia, where she whines about the weather for most of the year while secretly admitting she'll probably never move.

http://www.louisamasters.com

Printed in the USA
CPSIA information can be obtained
at www.ICGtesting.com
CBHW032346030524
8049CB00008B/112